From America's Heartland to America's Dreamland

Arden K.'s climb to literary superstardom began with a searing exposé of six naked cheerleaders at Beloit High. Then it was on to the Big Apple, where a lot more than cheerleaders turned up naked . . .

Belinda Blumright: an aspiring actress who dropped by for coffee and ended up giving the most inspired performance of her life . . . on her back.

Bernie Guysman: a Brooklyn movie exec with a dream—to capture forever on the silver screen the gossamer beauty of love . . . between forty people.

Z: the most diabolically beautiful and evanescent woman since V.

Through it all, Arden K.'s destiny was to become a famous person in New York City. And the day his novel rocketed to the top of the bestseller list, his fate was cast as—

SON OF THE GREAT AMERICAN NOVEL

By James Fritzhand

"A first-rate storyteller"
West Coast Review of Books

SON OF THE GREAT AMERICAN NOVEL

James Fritzhand

AVON
PUBLISHERS OF BARD, CAMELOT AND DISCUS BOOKS

AVON BOOKS
A division of
The Hearst Corporation
959 Eighth Avenue
New York, New York 10019

First Avon Printing, June, 1978

AVON TRADEMARK REG. U.S. PAT. OFF. AND IN
OTHER COUNTRIES, MARCA REGISTRADA,
HECHO EN U.S.A.

Printed in the U.S.A.

for
Duff
Deborah
Timothy
three friends

SON OF THE GREAT AMERICAN NOVEL

James Fritzhand

"All is pretension, for there are no beginnings and even fewer endings."

—JEREMY HABERMAN

Chapter 1

AT TEN O'CLOCK in the morning, toward the end of May and also the day after Arden K. had taken a trip, he awoke with a dead arm. The alarm clock had not disturbed his slumber. Not even set at its appointed task, he could not blame the rude awakening of consciousness on that simple and guileless machine. All through the night, the dawning, the morning, the faintly illuminated dial had watched his body shifting, searching for womb warmth, kicking back the covers and then drawing them up again over his head. The clock was electric with a guaranteed Swiss-style movement, plugged into a socket behind the bed. It made very little extraneous noise, announcing the movements of its hands—witness to the honest labor and revolution of its class—by a low-pitched and barely audible hum.

Like so: HUMMMMM...

Nevertheless, Arden felt a tender affection for the Baby Ben soft-glo dial. It had been manufactured in Elgin, Illinois, not too many miles from where he had spent his sturdy rustic boyhood. No, it was not the clock that had urged his eyes to open. For Arden, leaving the fetal shadows of wrinkled damp linen (avoiding synthetics whenever possible), had heard the traffic backing up along Second Avenue. Horns shrieked—diesel-fed rocs in an aviary without bars. Little mini taxi bloops and blurps and extended hand-tooled luxury vehicles, all these protesting with various degrees of impatience the slow

11

course of events down the East Side. Arden K. heard their sounds of multiplied violence, manic irritation, and he turned over, groggy, feeling not at all like himself. But there was something in his bed, an unwanted and rejected foreign body, and with this realization his eyes opened wide, or at least as far as the *levator palpebrae superioris* muscles would allow. He looked closely. A piece of meat resting humbly along his side, doing no apparent harm nor causing injustice to anyone. He looked down and found his arm, the skin blanched, creased with the weight of his torso and his thousand and one Dali dreams. A piece of kosher meat with all the blood drained off, ready to be salted.

With the one hand that was still alive he prodded the limb, pinched the unresisting flesh and felt nothing. The skin had no consistency and reminded him of clay, grist for the potter's wheel. He threw his legs over the side of the bed and dragged the unwilling appendage along with him.

"Help! I have a dead arm!" he cried out in a tiny child's voice that he supposed was terribly amusing, swinging the pins-and-needles wrist and fingers back and forth, rocking them to attention to get the blood moving, urging the life fluid into action and also thinking how inappropriate were his first remarks of the day, how his official biographer would find dozens of unmeant symbols running rampant through his audible prose. "What can you do with a dead arm?" he asked himself, catching hold of the day's rhythm in the creak of the floor boards beneath his feet. "Sell it to Shylock. Send it to the Pentagon as my token protest against the industrial-military complex."

He went to the window, brushed aside the sleeping cat as if it were so much dust, and looked outside. A late-morning sun climbing in its arc toward high noon, fit for two bowlegged Titan warriors engaged in a Cheyenne street duel, filtered through the shreds of torn-tissue-paper clouds, its edges blurred and indistinct.

"Another day, another Dolly," he moaned, turning his eyes across an ocean—a mere instant in trapped time—and wondering if Bob Hope and Martha Raye would finally be entertaining the boys stateside this coming Christmas. Then he blinked into the present and cast a glance at his desk, almost embarrassed when he came in contact with the pile of unread manuscripts. He let the curtain fall back into place, reached down to run his hand through the sooty fur along the cat's knobby spine.

"I hate you New York! Your whole system sucks!"

For the moment, he was satisfied.

Once inside the bathroom he placed both hands on the basin and peered into the mirror. A purist at heart, he rubbed away the flecks of dried shaving cream along the glass surface, surveying the wreckage of the past twenty-four hours. He remembered the bowl of carnelian colored punch, the silver-plated dipper, the mind games.

"Oh Christ," his favorite basso oath accompanied now by a dribble of stale saliva sluicing out of the corner of his mouth, his hands beginning to tremble as he stared at the passage of time, at the deep pockets, the Cricetusian pouches of night color—purple and blue—which hung disconsolately from beneath each blood-encircled eye.

"Thirty years old, old man, and what in God's name have you got to show for it? An original Warhol litho and a set of books from The Heritage Club."

Thinking, Who needs buckram when the world's gone plastic?

"Yep," he concluded with the same tone of disbelief, "someone's going to have a shitfit around here, an absolute shitfit that's all I can say."

It was all Owsley's fault, that little unseen yet fondly remembered man who now, somewhere in places hidden, could not even begin to understand the consequences of his chemical, his alchemic madness and skill. Rather than gold it was blue this time, filled with joy and cheer for all

13

the believing and wanting children, Arden K. not being an obvious exception. And now this magic—made potent across a continent—lent itself for mass sense orgies psychedelic shenanigans. The carnelian-colored liquid and a shy look of fond preference for jaded and forbidden things flashed across his face.

While somewhere back at the ranch in Long Beach, along the San Andreas Fault, a masked king straddled an unwilling bull, heading out to sea in search of wine and the last of the perfect waves. Unknowing, Arden could not be moved to tears. This morning he saw little beyond the confines of his rooms.

Searching out his soul in the medicine cabinet mirror, his features broken by the interface between two sliding slabs of glass, Arden recalled how his eyes had looked, that strange demonic glazed and dilated stare that had scared the superintendent of his building, who, arranging plastic bags of garbage early on a Monday morning, was presented by the sight of one of his tenants skipping down a quiet six A.M. street. "Hello and a good good morning to *you!*"

But my eyes were freaky then and the old man doesn't remember what happens to him from one day to another, he decided, lowering his white winter body onto the frosty seat. Wincing as his baby-soft skin, which ran in the family, made contact, then relaxing, turning an eye back to the tank shelf, mentally rearranging the comb and brush, the water glass with its faint lees of stannous fluoride, the bottle of oral antiseptic, the box of decorator-styled tissues. Mentally shifting their positions in search of the...aha!...he grinned. In search of the universal symbol, the universal truth! He stopped concentrating on the problem of his ablutions and closed his eyes.

He saw it all now: a wide rounded spine, backbone for a million thoughtful words. And he saw the cover, a dust jacket printed on glossy stiff white paper. The front side would picture him sitting on the tank shelf of a white toilet, his head buried in his hands, his feet—unable to decide on bare toes or shoes—resting on the seat. Nothing else. The back side would have him photographed in the same position, only this time he would be looking straight ahead, the trace of a cosmic Arden smile playing for all its worth upon his face. And the title. Above where it would say "An Epic by Arden K. Hoffstetter," he saw the heavy modern letters. FLUSH. Suddenly blinded by the clarity of this vision he jerked his eyes open, lifted his hands above his head, crying aloud, "Mother Hoffstetter, what did you do to deserve a child like this?"

Who was Arden K.?

No one knew for sure, but he was the type of person who could spend an hour sitting at his desk, hunched over his typewriter, his fingers poised in flight, unmoving, trying to decide if he should use the present tense and write: "Who *is* Arden K.?" or employ the past tense and the softer sounding *was*.

Ostensibly, he was a reader. That is, he supported himself by reading manuscripts on a freelance basis. He farmed three or four big city publishers, picking up unsolicited novels from their fast-growing slush piles. He read them, wrote a brief critical report on plot, characters, construction, and marketability and thus earned for himself upward of twenty dollars a shot. Of course, Arden did not intend to spend his life reading other people's works. When he had come to the big city after graduating from college he had fashioned himself a latter-day Youngblood Hawke. But after nearly eight years of creative suffering, he was still without an agent, still without a publisher, and still without a finished work.

Arden K. was a bright young man, a high school nominee for "Boy Most Likely to Succeed." Modest, unassuming, with the kind of bland good looks that mothers approved of, our aspiring novelist found comfort in his dreams, in reveries which led him down the paths of literary glory. In giving up Horatio Alger, he had yet to discover Sammy Glick. Life, as far as he was concerned, was not a problem. When other people bemoaned their fate, their constant unhappiness, he would only smile, secure in the belief that he had touched upon the perfect method of existence. He liked to think that he was able to see the unity and profound ecology of events when others could only glimpse a portion, a single strand of the complex interweaving system. Thus, he fancied moving on two levels—seeing and living inside and yet still able to stand aloof and observe it all from the outside. Arden K. was the man that no one had dared to write about: the archetypal fence-sitter, the prototypal fence-straddler.

Preparing scrambled eggs in his kitchen, a meal not out of hunger but only of habit, the effects of the electric punch and the neon moo still circulating within his system—random organic acid molecules bouncing off the capillary walls—Arden moved his hands mechanically. He broke two large duck eggs—this week's market special—into a bowl obtained from cereal coupons, splashed in some cream, added paprika, dill, lemon and pepper, and green onion. McCormick & Company was thankful for his patronage. The butter was losing its clarity, turning brown in the skillet and he poured the well-beaten mixture into the pan, dreaming absently of a recipe for curry he had read about in *The Chocolate Egg*. The muffin was buttered and the eggs drying into large yellow and green-flecked curds when he heard something being pounded above his head. There was no window in the kitchen, and through the air vent above the gas range he heard a voice asking,

"Are you up yet?"

It was the girl who lived in the upstairs apartment. Anxious to tell someone about his most recent adventure,

Arden tilted his head toward the metal grating. "Want some coffee?" he yelled.

"I'm on macrobiotics," he thought he heard her reply. "But mind if I watch you eat?"

"Just don't you dare bring Yossel. He'll kill the cat."

A moment later, the food already growing cold on the table, she opened his door with her spare key. (It is wise to note that the latter had been provided for use in emergencies and not intimacies.) "I don't know what you have against my darling baby," she said brightly, deciding in a flash that the mood was not right for low-keyed openers. Coming into the kitchen she swirled around like a frustrated ballerina in her floor-length black slip, then paused with a hand on her hip. "Whatt a dumpp!"

"Sit," he intoned, ignoring her flawless imitation of one of his more favorite stars and motioning to a chair. He loaded his fork with breakfast food. "Your Yossel is no innocent. Kinkajous are vicious and irascible little beasts. One swipe of his claws and the cat'll be ready for the taxidermist."

"Touchy, touchy, touchy," pouring a cup of coffee, temporarily removing herself from the obligations of her diet and sniffing inquisitively. "Chicory? Are we that strapped for funds?"

"Mother wrote that it's better for the system. Supposed to promote regularity. Besides, caffeine results in long-range genetic defects. You know," swinging the empty fork in the air like a pointer, "acts like a mutagen."

"No dirty talk so early in the day."

"It's almost eleven," said Arden with unflinching exactitude.

"Anyway," the girl told him, "Yossel's nails are drying." The last was justified with a peculiar attempt at a pout. She strained to catch the reflection of her mouth in the gleaming surface of the toaster. "White platinum. Only the best for my baby."

17

"Wonderful," he said, looking down at his plate with a frown. He might as well have been eating paper; his mouth was slack, all the taste buds gone into temporary retirement.

"So, Mister Great American Novelist, how's the *opus magnus* coming along? Still within striking distance, I hope." Through the synthetic material of her slip he saw that she was naked, and Arden lusted with growing fervor after the two pert protuberances now revealing themselves as the girl sat down and brought the cup to her gaping red wound of a mouth.

"I think you're swell," he whispered, his eyes glazed over like two marbles, not even knowing that to millions of American housewives he resembled, just for this moment, Bob Richardson in all his penultimate crunch-flaked glory.

"Stop drooling." The carmine sore healed magically, transforming itself into a somber slash of colorless ingratitude.

"That's your basic problem," Arden replied. "You lack emotion."

"What I may lack in feeling, dearheart, I make up for in my rare ability to capture a pose, a phrase of melody."

"Drink your java, baby, or I'll smash a grapefruit across your moniker." He wasn't bothered. He knew she would fail, as usual, to understand.

What we have here is a failure to materialize. But that can be easily rectified.

Who was the girl, the dame with the coal-tar dyed lips?

An academic question, for she was well known by all the Hungarian meat dealers along Second Avenue, from 79th Street clear up to 86th. She was Yorkville's flower (as that section of Manhattan is called), and the purveyors of wurst, the vendors of Central European refugee condiments and goulash staples—prime ingredients for the neo-Horst Wessel movement—held her in considerable esteem.

This near-child, somewhere lurking, a caged vanity between the ages of twenty and twenty-five, was born Brunhilda Blumerreich. Supposedly, her father's third cousin twice removed was the opera star Regina Resnik who had, also supposedly, once played the Wagnerian role with great success. The name had been a source of increasing irritation to the growing child and once having achieved adolescent emancipation—moving out of her father's countinghouse so that he could no longer claim her as a dependent deduction on his income tax—she had changed it to Belinda. Jane Wyman had also done the right thing, she had thought, the moment her new identity was crystallized. Later and now she signed her checks Belinda Blumright. To those who were unfamiliar with the *nom de plume*, it invariably came out with a lisping sneer.

Fitzgerald would have called her "a girl like a record with a blank on the other side," but Arden was immensely fond of his neighbor. The two of them shared a common aspiration, fame. Arden through his writing, Belinda through her quest for the perfect audience, the hypnotized begging-for-more mass of quivering flesh. The heterogeneous made one, homogenized humanity wowing her on for song after song.

Alas, at this very moment, before our story even takes off and God only knows if it ever will, even Off-off Broadway was not yet ready for her considerable disarray of talents.

He cleared the dishes, rather annoyed that Belinda had not volunteered to wash them. If he had said something to her about it, she would only have shrugged. "I only had coffee. Whaddaya want from my life? Blood?"

Thankful for small things, ungiven favors, he was still

pleased with her. She wore no zippers, no hooks or clasps or unsightly buttons. So much the better.

"The old man confided in me on the stairs..." she began.

"A questionable honor, don't you think?"

She stamped her foot on the floor, signal for him to refrain from interfering. "Zibrovski thinks you're a drug freak."

"The super?"

"That's right. What happened last night?" She was eating Oreo cookies, separating each chocolate wafer and licking off the vanilla cream with her prehensile tongue.

"I went on a trip," wondering if he should have been wearing braces, suspenders made to hook his thumbs around, stick out his chest and beam with fire-fighting pride.

"Where? Bayonne or Bay Ridge?" making a face so that her nose seemed to wrinkle up like a louver door. "I wish I had a big nose. I just hate this little pug of a thing." Belinda paused to see what the world had given her, crossing her eyes and making Arden burst into laughter.

"My dear, when one goes on a trip, it isn't necessarily with a geographic destination in mind. There are other ways to go places to get from here to there."

"Tell me about it," came her cyanide reply. "And while you're at it, do me a favor and don't talk like you're writing a book or something hard-covered. Just tell me what happened without the mixed-media metaphors." Running her tongue over her lips she slouched down in her chair, Yogi exercises making her a perfect instrument of attentive communication.

"One of my friends, my...uh, many faultless acquaintances, gave himself a little unbirthday party. Acid and mescaline, darling."

"More flower-children games, right? I don't need any artificial devices to expand my consciousness. Do you know how many chromosomes you must have broken last night? Your offspring may grow up looking like seals."

"Perhaps." Unperturbed Arden went on, "but we all drank fruit punch laced with LSD and other goodies and the result, the result was exquisite." He threw his hands into the air, always more histrionic than was his nature whenever Belinda was near. "At first," slipping down along the wall and hugging his knees to his chest, "it was as if someone was pulling my neck apart, making me smile. Waves of smoothness came over me and I was filled with an absolutely incredible sense of good will. Velvet smelled like gardenias; the walls began to vibrate with a pattern of spinning iridescent wheels and the music—wow! The notes were wrapping themselves around my throat. I could see the molecules in my hands, glowing pentagons and octagons, as if I had entered my own body and, the best part of all, no ego. Can you imagine, not having an ego? Suddenly I wasn't worrying about Arden Hoffstetter. I was just attuned to my surroundings."

Her mouth drew itself into a gash, the ends turned down. "Next case." She projected great pain into her carefully made-up eyes. "And what if kids read this? You'll have the whole country screaming for your life. Come on, Arden, this isn't any way to start a novel. Can't you be a little more innovative?"

"I'm trying, so the least you could do is listen impartially. Do you know that walking down Madison Avenue at dawn, it was as if I'd never lived here. Everything was so clean and spotlessly new...."

"That's because it rained last night."

He ignored the interruption. "The streets shone. All the pigeons I so adamantly despise cooed like divine apparitions, it was that nice. I'm telling you that my apartment didn't even seem to belong to me. And all morning as I tried to catch some winks I kept having these Dali-like dreams, with geometric girls sodomizing themselves and landscapes melting into pieces of a face encased in bubbles."

"If you don't watch out, sweetie, it just might happen to you," she said with a sneer, leaving him to ponder the threat of a most penetrating fate. "And I suppose you intend to try it again?"

"Maybe in a month or two," he told her, cooling off. "It was just a baby trip, sweetheart, only two or three hundred mikes." He looked at her eagerly, a child waiting for his teacher's compliment.

Belinda yawned. Unmindful of Arden's disappointment she opened her mouth wide, displaying bits of chocolate in the corners of her teeth. "While you were off in never-never land, I was sitting upstairs being abused."

"By whom?"

"By who? By myself. By humanity. By the walls that need a good paint job. I suppose you think I like playing mother, maid, and hostess to a South American carnivore. Well, I do and I don't. Kinkajous are a little limited when it comes to demonstrativeness. Anyway, Saturday was M-day and I fluffed it."

Arden cocked his head to one side. "Go on."

"I hate that mischievous smile which plays upon your face," she said, continuing in the same tone with, "I wish I could. There's not another thing I wouldn't enjoy more than to go on and become the toast of the town. Only baby, it was M-day with a capital T and the bald soprano fluffed it."

"Fluffed what?" he asked the required question, following the usual formats when it came to this sort of thing.

"Fluffed it. Blew it," she whispered. "The tryout. That's what I've been trying to tell you. The audition."

"For what?"

"Questions," she replied bitterly. "You're the goddamn pasha of hassles. Someday someone will put you in your place with all your ridiculous questions. Listen! Merrick the maker or breaker is doing a new musical. He's got a book already written, with Bernstein doing the music—

giving it that old Lennie touch—and Marianne Moore doing the lyrics."

"A real headliner, eh?" hoping he had chosen a correctly theatrical choice of terms.

"A blockbuster. It's all about the life and times, in bed and out, of Captain Tom Thumb. You know, P. T. Barnum's circus dwarf. He's got Robert Joffrey and Jerome Robbins to do the choreography, Marc Chagall to work on the sets and it's going to bust the Alley wide open. I mean, this is going to be a *class* show. No *shlock* job, that you can be sure of. So anyways, I went down to the theater...."

"To try out for the lead?" he asked with a look of astonishment.

"Natch. Who'd think they'd stoop so low as to go after an actual freak." On a lower register her voice told him, "But they did. Arden—every dwarf and cretin in the five boroughs and Long Island besides was there. It was like an experiment in terror. I was practically booed off the stage when I crawled out on my knees to sing "Happy Birthday." All these little midget monsters were gnashing their teeth and hissing. Some moron had a Mongoloid idiot strapped into a Barca-lounger right there in the middle of the aisle, it was that sick. I lost my shoe and blew my cool," she whimpered. "It's just another case of the old Blum-wrong luck all over again."

"Don't be disheartened," Arden called out as she moved off into the bedroom with a pair of dragging shoulders, his voice gathering conviction as he plucked tiny wiggly shadows from between the creases of her silky black gown. "I'm sure you would have made a great Thumb!" he yelled after her. Then he picked himself off the floor and followed, led on by the signals he received from the syncopated sway of her lower and better half.

"Uncontrollable, like a beast," he admonished himself.

Already blood was being impounded—through no fault of his own—within the vascular spaces of his

corpora cavernosa. Nerves were busy flickering neon-lit
charges of power and waves of acetycholine began doing
their job, functioning perfectly as parasympathetic
impulses passed from the sacral portion of his spinal cord
via the pelvic splanchic nerves. What dirties! Indeed, the
nervi erigentes were getting quite worked up. The penile
arteries were dilatating and the exiting veins were being
compressed mercilessly in the process. Arden's pulse
quickened as Belinda leaned over the bed and began to
play with the cat, fondling the fur with long tapering
candle fingers.

"Why don't you give her a name?" the undiscovered
superstar wanted to know. "It doesn't seem fair and
anyway, it's been done before."

He whispered, "What has?" His lips were suddenly
puffy and his blood pressure rose with each breath he
took.

"Capote used a cat in one of his little books and called
it just that. Cat. Give her a name."

"What name? I detest people who name their cats after
figures in mythology. Likewise for those pet lovers who
insist on being cute with little christening parties for
Ralph or Sam. It's enough that parents are naming their
kids Poindexter or Ladybird Shapiro."

"I suppose you think Yossel is not good enough," she
said in a huff.

"Kinkajous are not cats," he added quickly. The last
thing he wanted to do was antagonize her. Not now. Not
at this crucial Arden moment. He did not want to offend.
Led on by the needs of his increasingly complex
organism, he sat down beside her and ran his fingers along
her back. He thought of an opening line, seeing scenes
from a thousand late-night movies. *Did I ever tell you that
you were irresistible?* Not strong enough. Too banal. Or
how about *charming, divine, inscrutable.* Or *I've been in
love with you ever since you became the spoiled little rich
girl who lived down the block.* Or *you're my American*

dream so how about coming out and playing in my sandbox? But she'd miss all the precious allusions. *You have a body like a Botticelli goddess so why don't you open your shell so we can spoon on the hot sauce?*

She looked at the fellow who had awakened during the first paragraph, her eyes compressed into two glaring slits. She looked at this fellow whom the world would learn to love and realized that a little bit of torrid foreplay always kept the reader's eye from straying. "What are you thinking about, Mr. Hoffstetter?"

"Call me Arden," lapsing into a banana-filled daydream.

"Arden," she called softly. "What's going on inside, plumface?"

"Prurient things. Unmentionable lascivities. The same thing described so boringly on page 334 of *Couples.* Why don't we get under the covers? I detect a noticeably unpleasant chill in the room. Besides, there's too much dust in the air."

"That's because your windows aren't weather-proofed. Tell Zibrovski to put in putty."

That's just what I am, he said to himself. "I'm sure he has enough problems of his own without having to worry about my paltry domestic needs."

"Aren't we the prince among men," she laughed. Then the cat jumped off the bed, made a sound like a bubble popping and Arden, forever aware of signals and outside influences, thrust his tongue between Belinda's lips, tasting Suddenly Last Summer lipstick on his revitalized fungi-form papillae.

"I suppose this is what comes of being an over-solicitous neighbor," she murmured, resigning herself to the pressure of his body against her length and breadth, as well as the insistent tremble of his muscular legs.

"Why resist the inevitable?" Arden K. asked in a whisper, the impulses carried from his papillae and up into his brain where he soon enough realized he was tasting salt and soft downy body hair.

The black slip slipped to the floor and with his mouth still glued to hers he shifted their bodies into a more rewarding position, resting her head on the pillow. "Promise you'll be gentle," a Metro girl pleaded with all the lust the Code of Decency would allow, her heavy false eyelashes fluttering under the weight of sound-stage arc lamps.

"I hope it isn't feathers. I'm an allergic child," Belinda warned him.

As if to soothe her troubled histamines, he wiped her dampening brow. "Foam rubber. Even though I'm basically opposed to synthetics, down is still beyond the present limitations of my budget."

"Good boy."

She reminded him of a girl he had seen in a television doctor show, her head encased in impressive crisp white bandages, looking up sweetly at the face of the young blond intern, her eyes begging and asking, "Will I make it? Will I ever dance again?" And in a thousand and one pieces of forbidden Victoriana, mental voyeurs licked their slobbering lips and followed the sentences and paragraphs of gamahuching and doing a St. George, of delicious bouts, deflorations, and lubricious mounts.

His body, Arden K.'s sacred vessel, reacted, reflex building on reflex.

The tissues elongated, distended, and stiffened. At the same time a layer of muscle investing the posterior portion of the corpora cavernosa constricted, restricting the outflow of blood. So far so good, for soon after the more delicate connective tissue trabeculae of the corpus spongiosum and glans began to become engorged with trapped blood. The head enlarged, poked forward without respect for the laws of public morality and the walls of the urethra swelled with unbridled longing. The meatus and sensory end organs, now stimulated beyond their wildest middle-class dreams and in great heat, began to convey impulses to the spinal cord via the pudental nerves.

The accessory glands quivered and went into action, deciding: "Fans, it's time to wrap up the ball game."

Those twin peas, the small but significant Cowper's glands, readied their ducts. Moving into the urethra and passing into the engorged bulb of the corpus spongiosum came an alkaline viscid fluid, a mucoid secretion that when mixed with three parts hashish was able to induce second degree hallucinations. It washed along the walls, lubricating the tissue and removing any traces of injurious urine.

Not to be undone, mean little monster that it was, the prostate gland which, in later years, would give Arden considerable discomfort, now began secreting a thin and milky fluid. Acid phosphatase, citric acid, and a fibrinolysin poured along the urethral walls, neutralizing the vaginal acidity, doing its job to insure motility and fertility—much to Belinda's chagrin—of the as-yet-unleashed spermatozoa.

Arden pumped on, licking Belinda's ear lobes—also red with increased supply of blood. He felt his heart pounding, the temperature of his body scaling to new thermometric heights. "Are you ready?" he moaned, trying not to be selfish but unable to hold back much longer and wishing for this minute that he was still a straddling lad of twenty-one.

She thrust forward, matching him stride for stride as they drew into the last stretch. "A little more. Soon. Very soon."

The suffocating homunculi waited with growing impatience, one hundred million heads and tails per milliliter jostling each other in the ampulla of the ductus deferens. Things were reaching a head. Molecules of fructose, pushy and aggressive as was their nature, joined the already-crowded chamber and the tails began to move. Thank God the seminal vesicles had done their job!

Suddenly he could contain himself no longer. He grunted out loud, "I'm..."

Peristaltic waves moved along, followed by rhythmical contractions of the smooth muscle layers of the testes, epididymides, seminal vesicles and prostate gland. Rhythmical sympathetic impulses left the lumbar nerves and passed through the hypogastric plexus. There was no stopping him now.

Unable to wait another second, the bulbocavernosus muscles contracted, innervated to the breaking point by fibers traveling in the busy pudendal nerves. Carbohydrates, mucin, proteins, salt—all the fluids from the testes, epididymides, seminal vesicles, prostate, and Cowper's glands—this and all the lashing little boys and girls now released with slithering violence. Pandemonium as the urethral orifice felt their outward passage. At intervals of eight-tenths of a second the muscles continued to contract.

Arden shuddered, "I'm...ahhhhhhh," and he grabbed her tightly with a pulse of 143 and his blood pressure gone to 210. Sweat ran down his sides as 3.37 milliliters of semen rushed away from him. With the last contraction, the final shudder, Belinda joined in the pleasure of his ecstasy and shortly afterward they both lay contentedly exhausted on the damp sheets of Arden's bed.

"You're...unbelievable," he grinned as the imprisoned blood was now slowly released and the vascular spaces began collapsing to their unused detumescent proportions. "A wonderful girl." He flashed his universal master-novelist smile and kissed her gently on each check.

Chapter 1½

DRIVING due south and careful to observe all the rules of road etiquette, a pleasant half-hour journey after a Sunday morning well spent at the Beloit First Congregationalist Church, you will enter upon the domain of Arden K. Hoffstetter's bulk of experience. Not far from the Wisconsin-Illinois border there is a little town, a self-contained and prospering community, that—at first glance—reminds the casual visitor of the set used for the series of Andy Hardy movies, loved and cherished by all those who remember them. Arden grew up in a two-storied frame house which had no need to be surrounded by an electrically charged cyclone fence. The house was on Elm Street, right off Cherry Drive, a short walk to Main and State Streets, the Bijou Theater, Pop River's Malt Shoppe and the Able-bodied Emporium.

We drove into town after hearing a thoroughly delightful and rewarding sermon in Beloit, prepared to gather background material for our official unauthorized (though sanctioned) biography of Arden K. Hoffstetter, also known as Wisconsin's Wonderkid. Our first stop was on Elm Street, where we hoped for an audience with Arden's mother, the former Blossom Larkin. We were not disappointed, for the now-widowed Mrs. Hoffstetter shares the same brand of gracious effusiveness and hospitality as does her son.

The attractively well-preserved matron came to the door in an Alice-blue dress with a dolman sleeve. She is still active in community affairs, sings in the church choir, and is known throughout the county for her prize-winning anemones, evidences of which could be seen on every level surface in the house. Indeed, she shares the same fondness for fresh-cut flowers as does her talented son, and told us that if the stems are crushed every day and the water changed as well, anemones can prove to be quite serviceable blooms. As we sat in her cozy gleaming kitchen, our hands, pencils, and pads resting on a shining oilcloth-covered solid rock maple table, Mrs. Hoffstetter poured us decaffeinated coffee with quiet assurance.

"Arden was always an individual," she began after the cream and sugar had been dispensed. "Not that he was a Communist or anything. Heavens no! Just that my boy always wanted more from life than our town could offer."

Do you remember anything in particular during his early and formative years which would indicate or foreshadow in any way this feeling of alienation from his surroundings?

"Well," she thought a moment, absently brushing back a strand of blue-tinted hair. "When our Arden was in high school an editorial came out in the local paper—that's Mort Clark's *Weekly Fanfare*. Mort was my late husband's second cousin on his mother's side, although he refused to acknowledge it in his lifetime. The Clarks and the Hoffstetters have never gotten along all too well. Of course, the Larkins weren't much better. But, as I was saying," she went on, looking slightly embarrassed, "there was this editorial condemning the... you know." She stopped short, tittering slightly so that the smooth skin in her cheeks turned pink (a pleasing contrast to the blue of her dress). "You know, those Eastern beatnik people. That was about in 1957, a year or two after Arden's father died, and just seven years almost to the day that my late husband was refused membership in the Masons. Well, as it were, Arden wrote the *Fanfare*—without my knowledge or consent mind you—a very strongly worded reply to their accusations, stating that Jesus was Jewish...would you believe! and had long hair too and that he was also the original Communist. I don't know where the boy got his ideas, or who he took after because they certainly don't come from my side of the family. Every five years my sister and I make a pilgrimage to Marion, Ohio, just to lay a wreath on our beloved President Harding's memorial.

"I tell you, the disturbance that letter caused around here was just not to be believed. Someone, though I suspect it was a disgruntled office-seeker from the wrong side of the tracks, threw a rock at our window, and I kept getting these threatening phone calls. They were ready to burn a cross outside on the front lawn and for the first time in my life, may the Lord strike me down if I'm not telling the truth, I was afraid for my person." She put down her cup and opened her eyes a fraction wider than was her way. "I had to lock my doors each night it got so bad."

"But Arden was a good boy, yes, he was always respectful to his mother. He wrote an apology to the paper and the whole thing just quieted down and people sort of forgave him for his misguided ways, being as he was still a youngster and all."

How do you feel about his sudden rise to literary fame?

"Well," she began, turning her eyes away and gazing beyond our faces to the line of wash drying brightly in the back yard. "Well...I haven't gotten around to reading the book yet. Three thousand pages is quite a lot to go through and I still haven't finished *Gone With the Wind*. Some of my friends have taken a peek at the copy Arden sent me, but the library won't stock it and there's no place in town that sells it, no place to buy books for that matter. If you want to buy a copy you have to go clear across the state line," pointing her finger vaguely and slightly right of center.

Then her face brightened as she handed us another

sweet roll. "But I'm glad Arden's happy and healthy, and thankful he's doing something that makes him feel useful. That's all we can ask out of life, isn't it sirs? Just a little peace and a bit of happiness, a quiet place to spend our years."

We left Mrs. Hoffstetter's with a bunch of freshly cut anemones, promised to relay her greetings to her son ("Ask him just to drop me a picture postcard from time to time. Views of the skyline are so nice, don't you think? Gosh, what's a mother to do? And make sure to remind him to brush after every meal. His father died with the best set of teeth in the county," she beamed.), got into our car and headed down State Street to the High School.

When Arden K. had been enrolled as a day student, there had been much talk of changing its name to the Joseph R. McCarthy Memorial High School for Boys and Girls. But the town council lacked the funds to authorize the appropriate changes in designation, what with the high cost of printing new stationery and all, and so it still stands today as the Branch 3 Normal High School or as the kids call it, Branch.

Our visit had been carefully arranged beforehand and we were not surprised at being met at the door by a cortege of students including reporters from Branch's weekly newspaper, the *Branch Buzz*, the Branch Homecoming Queen (a lovely little freckled child named Mary Ellen White), the strapping captain of the football team (the Branch Bombers), and the president of the Student Council (the latter being roughly equivalent to our Eastern G.O.'s or General Organizations).

"I'd sure like to make it to the big city," Mary Ellen confided with a million dollar smile. "I've been to Milwaukee and once to Chicago but I understand it's nothing like the real thing."

We patted her on the head, answered a few more questions and were soon led directly to the office of Mr. Henry Ackerley.

SON OF THE GREAT AMERICAN NOVEL

A word of explanation is in order. Mr. Ackerley had been Arden K.'s English teacher, faculty adviser to the drama group which put on the disastrous Hoffstetter play (for a full account see: R. Wreid, "The Branch Blues or Main Street Disinterred," *American Dramaturgy,* Vol. 11, pp. 123–131) during Arden's senior year, and current president of the Chamber of Commerce. Under his able and avuncular leadership the town has undergone a revitalized economic program, luring industry to its spacious building sites and progressive Christian way of life. To date, Mr. Ackerley's accomplishments include the opening of two Dairy Freeze enterprises, an authentic ethnic restaurant—Bill McBride's Italo-American Pizzeria—as well as plans for a Chinese hand laundry and a well-chaperoned drive-in movie.

Henry Ackerley is a warm and fulsome gentleman with graying temples and a sound handshake, somewhat short-tempered but always candid in his observations and opinions of the world around him. We crossed the seal-brown hallway, entered the faculty lounge, and settled into comfortable leatherette chairs. Dousing our ciga-rettes (Smoking Is Prohibited), we immediately began taking notes as he told us:

"Well, gentlemen, seems like one of our boys is causing quite a little stir *again,* wouldn't you say?" He smiled beneficently, waiting for our pens to catch up with him.

Again?

"Surely you are aware of Arden K. Hoffstetter's reputation. But frankly, I'm surprised he had the will power to write down all this dribble. As if anyone in their right mind would be interested in the machinations of a sewage disposal system." Clearing his throat, for he suffers from bronchial frogs, Ackerley drummed his fingers with nervous abandon on the arm of his chair.

What about his reputation?

"Arden was always a dreamer. Any of the local wags down at Pop River's place'll tell you of all the crazy

33

schemes he used to come up with. Plans for a row of peace trees and things like that. He daydreamed his way through high school and he undoubtedly daydreamed his way through college, although I haven't been able to get hold of his records to verify that point. Always an outsider, never content to follow the crowd, preferred rugby to football. Things like that. You know the type," he said, making a face that would have pleased the Elks Club. "I suppose it's all out in the open about the play we put on here during his last year. How I consented to allow it to be staged is still beyond the powers of human comprehension. But I did," he admitted weakly. "It set back Branch drama for a good five years, besides putting my tenure in tremendous jeopardy."

Have you read Flush?

"I've read some of the big-city reviews, but when a man still hasn't gotten around to *War and Peace* or *Les Misérables*, he's not going to waste his time on some hefty piece of contemporary filth. How anyone allowed it to be published . . ."

Are you aware of the book's nomination for both the Pulitzer Prize and the National Book Award? Hoffstetter has already appeared twice on coast-to-coast television.

"So?" He looked annoyed, impatient and anxious to leave. "So did Oswald and look what happened to him." He leaned over in his chair as we followed his eyes roaming restlessly around the room. "But did the League of Christian Readers give it their endorsement? I should say not!" he cried out triumphantly. "That there book isn't fit to be read by the children *or* the adults of any God-abiding community. The big city can't dictate our public tastes, young men." Mr. Ackerley rose from his place and glared at us with unabashed hostility, there being no other kind available, almost shouting as he revealed, "Did you fellers know that Arden Hoffstetter was a C-average student? Did you know that?" Smiling with uncommon malice, he pointed an accusing finger and commanded,

"Write that down. Take *that* to your editor!" Then he stormed out of the room, slamming the door behind him. We had decided that it was unnecessary to tell him that we were working freelance.

Critics are prone to find similarities with the Hoffstetter novel and the works of other contemporary and classic writers. Although evidences of Joyce, Roth, and Dostoevsky have been meticulously exhumed from the pages of *Flush*, it is our belief that only one fellow writer cast his creative magic on Arden K.'s prose. The name of Jacob Ivan Haberman, alias Jeremy Haberman and now almost as well known throughout the haunts of the literati, is often bandied about by progressive commentators and raconteurs of the New Left. The Hoffstetter-Haberman school of writers that has grown up in recent years generally agree upon the dual influences each author made upon the other. It has been carefully verified that both men first met quite accidentally (although this too has come under fire from various qualified sources about which we can say little more at this time) at the home of a prominent literary patroness and lady of the arts. But we have found additional evidence to substantiate the view that Arden K. was intimately familiar with the Haberman style long before the latter's first novel was published.

The following, found in the Hoffstetter Archives now in possession of the Society Library of New York, is basic proof of Arden K.'s early respect and considerable admiration for the work of Jeremy Haberman. It is interesting to note also that his predictions concerning the future of this book were, if slightly exaggerated, still remarkably accurate. We include now for your edification a transcript of a reader's report Hoffstetter composed after reading Haberman's unsolicited manuscript, *The Great American Novel*.

"Writing with both passion and self-assuredness,

Jeremy Haberman has constructed what we feel is a brilliant piece of literary craftsmanship. His work is a mélange of contemporary problems of ethical morality, translated and fashioned around what will undoubtedly become one of the most talked about American novels in years.

"Tush Botwinick, ensconced in the antediluvian Big House of Ebony Hill Farms, struggles through unrelenting odds to find his identity and sense of self-worth. Without self-pity but with macabre power, each scene is skillfully built upon the next, carrying the reader through a frightening maze of singular events and astounding characterizations. Botwinick's stream-of-consciousness soliloquies, fragments reminiscent of Molly Bloom but reconstructed from images of his own tormented past, bring to light his basic oral-anal genital conflicts and resultant fears. Ego formation is symbolized by his contact with the mysterious Suzanne, a silver-lamé bitch goddess who comes to Ebony Hill in search of the perfect rapist. Other memorably viable personages include Tush's faithful valet, the West Indian Hippolyte Ramirez, and Botwinick's senile uncle—a demon figure if ever there was one.

"With extraordinary mastery, Haberman captures the nuances of American dialect. He is equally adroit in handling the ebbing *schticks* of Crown Heights verbiage as he is with the Afro-American metaphors of an emasculated West Indian. His re-creation of the Southern manor with its carefully rendered vision of decadent plantation life, mint juleps *et al.*, draws to mind no obvious similarities. His brand of Southern Gothic (if we dare call it that) has not been seen by this reader since the genre was first made popular.

"The book's one flaw is in its belief in the outstanding and inherent goodness of its central character. Although Botwinick's neuroses are appealing and characteristically the lot of twentieth-century man, we find that the author is unable to fully utilize the Freudian symbolism which is the one leitmotiv of the novel. Therefore, at the end of the work, we are strangely disappointed in Botwinick's solution to his 'blues,' finding it rather hard to believe that he would stay on at Ebony Hill Farms in sackcloth and ashes to eventually bury his uncle (and the sordid remains of his *own* past) beneath the chinaberry tree in the back garden.

"Other than this minor reservation, we have only superlatives to report. This book has been a long time coming and its arrival should be heralded as a milestone in the further compression of American literary styles. Indeed, the era of the plausible non-novel is upon us.

"With forceful marketing, the book stands an excellent chance of becoming a genuine dark horse in the race for best-sellerdom."

Chapter 2

ARDEN our hero, not so tall, dark, and handsome but filled with untapped bravado, looked at his labialove, Belinda—undiscovered pride of a nation gone mad with feckless abandon—and smiling with genuine good humor, declared, "I've got a hunch!"

"If it's Franco-American spaghetti for lunch, count me out."

Without flinching, he went on, "Have you ever been in love and wouldn't you really adore accompanying me into the afternoon?"

Belinda had changed into a chartreuse jumpsuit when she had gone back to her apartment to feed her faithful Yossel. Arden had made the bed and opened the shutters so that the curious might not feel disappointed should they happen to pass by his window. Then the girl had skipped and hopped the return trip, playing the talented gamester as she descended the stairs, and was now absorbed in watching Arden tie a knot in a brown-velvet bow tie. She addressed her reflection in the mirror.

"I once loved a small male child I saw stepping out of Bendel's with his mother. The sun shone on the glass door on a day not unlike this one and he was a somewhat Japanese child with a fishbowl haircut and blond pony hair. The most beautiful male palomino child I had ever seen up to that time. And once I craved the life and loves of Steve Canyon. But when I got older and found out through a friend that he was probably a fascist, all the feelings just withered away." She had said the words carefully, enunciating properly and with earnest persuasiveness. Now she was annoyed that she hadn't brought along her tape recorder to preserve the monologue.

"Have you ever loved a living person?" Arden asked, putting the unfinishing blasé touches onto the folds of his knotted cravat.

"I don't like you when you're serious. Reality is depressing."

"Reality," he exclaimed with passion, swinging his body around on the heel of his foot, "is only for the bravely actual."

"If I were a somebody you wouldn't call me a coward."

"I like your jumpsuit."

"Thanks," she sulked into a dusty corner. "It helps."

Arden trod swiftly across the linoleum-covered floor. "Won't you come with me? Please."

A strange look, one that he had never noticed before, came across her face, vanishing almost as quickly. "I have to see a man about a dog," she replied.

"You're putting me on."

"Think what you want to. I have to see a very important man about a dog."

"You're still putting me on, but at what time?" he persisted.

"Oh," shaking her head ambiguously from side to side. "Sometime later."

"Then come with me now. It won't take that long and you'll meet some important people, maybe a contact or two."

"Who?" She eyed him curiously, seeing herself, at the same time, brilliantly portraying the role of a spoiled and demented bastard child living alone in a house of rare imposture. Of course, she would have to lighten her hair and learn how to affect a Cockney accent. But it would be worth it, or so she thought.

"Movie moguls," he replied, not easily put off.

"Kingpins. Mr. Ferris who makes names out of nobodies," he went on with a casually studied toss of his hair all groomed smartly into place. "It might be the one chance you've been looking for."

"I'll go," she decided, "but I want you to know that I don't believe in the spoils system. I've got to make it on my own, from rung to rung even if I have to take the pratfalls and setbacks. Rung to rung until I've climbed the ladder." Her eyes dazzled and sent out sparks of method brilliance. "Until I've reached the top, the apex of glory and see the Great White Way groveling at my feet. Understand?"

Arden pushed her gently to the door, patted his jacket pocket to make sure he had not forgotten to take his keys, said good-bye to the cat and with a bag of garbage held with difficulty in two fingers, followed Belinda's tawny lime body out into the sunlight.

It was but a short time following noon and Hoffstetter felt sated. He had fed his stomach and his base parts, indulged in a reckless fantasy or three and was now eagerly looking forward to the interview he had arranged in Brownsville.

"Where are we going?" Belinda asked, squinting at the harsh shining sun but refusing to break down, to act like Sue Lyons in *Lolita* and don disfiguring disguising sunglasses.

"Brownsville."

"Brooklyn is so passé, so *fin de siècle*," she groaned.

"Decadence is the food of the gods," he countered neatly.

"No one but no one goes *there* anymore. It just isn't done. What if any of my future fans see me? They just wouldn't understand."

"Nevertheless, three million people can't be wrong. Besides, Brooklyn has been the scene of a great many novels that were capable of sustaining satisfaction in terms of a mass-market audience."

"Ya know, sometimes your appeal is rather limited,"

she decided, looking at him with the corner of her face showing beside black hair. "And ya talk funny, too."

"The truth hurts, doesn't it?" Arden K. asked without understanding.

"Only if it affects you personally."

A soon-forgotten lady in an unborn Dynel topper passed by with two cats on a rhinestoned leash. Arden stepped quickly aside and as he shifted position—Proust on Venetian flagstone—he recalled the reasons which had compelled him to move out of his first apartment. He had liked the idea of the garden in back, and for a few weeks he enjoyed the freedom of being able to take a chair into the yard, to sit and read aspiring works in the sunshine, to feel the breezes playing catch with his hair and hurrying him along from page to page, sentence fragment to mythological allusion, insistent in their windy demands. But at night it seemed as if all the neighborhood cats converged on the backyard fence. Cartoons had not prepared him for their nightly serenade; he gave up on the idea of throwing out old shoes (having none) and alarm clocks (having but one) at the shadowy forms which moved gracefully across the breadth of his plot of manicured grass. And when they began to call, to scream unnervingly at each other, Arden thought he heard in their voices the cries of helpless old and young women, moans and pleading sobs brought on by the ravages of burly thugs and attackers. With each successive scream he would rush frightened to his window, expecting to witness the throes of an unaided lady in acute distress. He wondered if the one time he would not go to the window, thinking it was only the cats up to their old tricks, there would actually be a rapist performing his act. If that were so, if Arden K. did not move to shout out a warning, if he did not reach for his Princess phone with its comforting nite-lite, the guilt would follow him long after the maggots had made peace with his unearthly remains. So Arden had decided that garden-apartment living, despite its much-heralded advantages, was not to his liking and he had found another set of rooms that faced the street with its safety etched in the lamplight, there being no imminent danger of molestation without the muffling aid of grass and darkness.

At the corner, waiting for the light to change, Arden and Belinda, youthful innocents at the very least, walked into the middle of a demonstration headed for direct police confrontation. A circle of marchers carrying protest signs walked in an orderly circle along Second Avenue, watched at a short but unrespectful distance by a squad of ten wary policemen.

"Who are these freaks?" Belinda asked with disgust, immediately resentful and suspicious of any body of people that moved with uniform purpose.

Arden eyed the crew-cutted, button-down mass. "American youth, disenchanted with the land of plenty," he said quietly, fearful that his comments would induce a backlash and yet disturbed by the silence of the demonstrators, their crisp display of well-coordinated precision. He turned to an onwatcher, a rumpled bystanding man without age or habit. "What do they want from my beautiful America?" he asked, so terribly and suddenly subdued that one would have thought there was a death in the family.

"Beats me," the gentleman replied with a frown. "Just looks as if they're interested in making trouble. As if we don't have enough going on around here. Let me tell you," he confided, leaning over and touching Arden's ear with his lips, "that in my day we wouldn't have tolerated such a disturbance. No siree. If they don't like it here they can get the hell out. Who needs 'em, anyway? Hopheads and degenerates. You can bet your boots on that."

Arden K. mumbled a thank you, overheard one of fuzz city's finest explaining to one of his brave cohorts in blue, "Dropouts from Moral Rearmament, Up With People, and the Crusade for Decency. Just remember, don't use the Mace until you see the whites of their eyes."

CELIBATE YOUTH AGAINST
CREEPING PERIL

RONALD REAGAN
SOFT ON COMMIES

MENDEL RIVERS
HAD THE RIGHT IDEA

DRAFT PERVERTS
TO MAKE STREETS SAFE

DIEGO RIVERA
PAINTS DIRTY PICTURES

Such was the gist of their placards. Blue eyes staring straight ahead into future disaster, unkissed android lips held tightly without emotion, carriage erect without a stoop of round-shouldered complacency.

"Hey officer," a watchful troubleshooter called out. "This here mothah called me a pinko." He rapped his knuckles on a recently tonsorialated head. "You gonna let a fairy like this get away wid abusing the everyday public?"

Perhaps the accent was a bit thick, shades of Slapsie Maxie Rosenbloom and the Hollywood of the thirties, but the point was made, for "Not on your life!" came the cry of the ten puffed to four hundred. "On your mark, get set, go!" Suddenly the line buckled and signs began to fly through the air. One smashed into the window of the Army-Navy Surplus Store and the owner came rushing out of his shop armed with a fire hatchet.

"Pogrom! Hitlerites! Rape! *Bondeet!*" screamed an elderly shopper caught in the melee, dropping her reinforced brown paper bag and rushing into the Hungarian Bakery with the remains of splattered eggs on her orthopedic shoes.

Indeed, Arden the writer saw all, watched gold and silver fillings and prize winning orthodontia crunched underfoot.

SON OF THE GREAT AMERICAN NOVEL

The cries of the scuffle echoed down the avenue and as the police moved into action, Arden grabbed hold of Belinda's bewildered arm and whisked her to safety.

"My hero," she should have said breathlessly, feigning a much-publicized swoon, her mascara blurred with the damp stain of chemically induced tears. Instead, his neighbor put her hands on her hips and stood watching the disturbance going on across the way. "That'll show those fuckers," she said without equivocation.

A gray cloud seemed suspended above the bleeding heads and packed display of random arms and legs. Coughing spread like an epidemic of yawning and Belinda's eyes watered over and she began to sniffle.

Society is basically unhappy, Hoffstetter observed. No one lets you make peace with your God.

But he would show them.

Soon. Very soon.

Already his idea of the media was gestating deep within the warmth of his cranial cavity. From the undimensionality of thought to the two-dimensionality of prose and the written word to the final statement, the last monumental step of crystallization: the three-dimensional mimicry of reality transposed to the silver screen. Panavision panoramas: final tribute to a man's own personal fantasies. To clothe his words into the living breathing bulk of human flesh—this was Arden K.'s singular dream, his consuming monomania and the ultimate meaning behind his quest for written perfection. To see his characters come alive for millions of admission-paying voyeurs, enacting events that had once been born inside his own head—this was Hoffstetter's as yet unrealized goal.

Each day I get closer, he told himself with growing confidence. Each day the page gap narrows and the road ahead seems clearer. Now, if I only had an ending...

"When they buy the movie rights to my novel, will you star in it?" he asked the girl he had brought along to replace his loneliness.

"You mean the female lead?"

Arden nodded his head.

"No."

"Why not?"

"I told you," tired of unremembered repetitions, "that I have to break in on the legitimate stage. Not out of a trunk. Not through friends, but on my own. What do you think I am, a two-bit honky? Listen baby, films come later." She lowered her heavy black lashes and glared at him with professional fervor. "First Broadway. After that, when I can write my own ticket anywhere, you can work something out with my agent."

"But you're not on Broadway and you don't have an agent."

"Pragmatist! Despoiler of virgin dreamers!" she yelled scornfully. "Don't dare to impose your two-cents worth of values on my subtly constructed way of life. If there's one thing I can't abide, can't stand in a person, it's being jealous of my talent and enormous gifts."

A paddy wagon was being filled with accumulated paddywhacks, loaded up with struggling bodies ruckusing and fracasing here and there in three-piece suits, gray and charcoal-brown herringbone predominating, as the two of them continued on their way to the subway.

Arden K. the para-professional reader was transformed at dusk into Arden K. the novelist, Arden K. the imaginative and sensual word gatherer. No cry of "Shazam!" or "Geewhiz!" broke through the air or rent the clouds over Yorkville asunder. There were no brightly colored tights and sweeping day-glo cape hidden in a recess of his closet, no snug-fitting vinyl boots or devices to foil the archcritics and antichrists of Big City. Nay; such things, such artificial contrivances, were not for our Arden. Nor did Hoffstetter pace around his living room making furrows of troubled meditation along the parquet floor. Creativity was not so difficult or fraught with the peril of lengthy contemplation.

Immediately after the six o'clock news, the supper dishes draining in the rubber-coated plastic tray on the sink, Arden made himself a pot of coffee, placed a pack of cigarettes within reach and began writing. The routine never varied. First he would read the pages he had written the night before. He would pen in corrections, making notes to himself along the narrow margins. Then he would either work on something entirely new or else revise one of the previous chapters. The first statement of his ideas came out on lined looseleaf paper. The second statement, greatly edited and hopefully improved, was typed on canary yellow second sheets. It was in this way that Arden was always working on two levels, two fronts of attack—rough draft and first rewrite. As our story opened, Arden K. had completed approximately 2,500 pages of second-draft canary yellow rewrite on the manuscript he had been working on for the past five years. He saw his labor—perhaps only another four or five hundred pages—finally drawing to a close as soon as he could think of an appropriate ending that would pull all the pieces of his work together.

Being an agreeable sort and not wishing to make enemies or offend unnecessarily, we shall answer your next question. What were all these words about? Isn't that what you want, what you are so anxious to know? For an answer, one must go back for a moment, hoping to capture an episode of time past.

As a small child, although he was somewhat taller than his peers, Arden was more inclined towards the *vita contemplativa* than the *vita activa*. Once, on a family outing that sped Mr. Hoffstetter's Packard Clipper into the hilly and mountainous reaches of northern Wisconsin, Arden had asked his parents, "How do the mountains work?"

He had seen the tree-covered hills rising in the distance, countless bare branches turning a faint and hazy purple with the approach of spring. The hills reminded him of

Indian haircuts with the naked winter trees forming a straight clipped line across the tops of the rounded peaks.

"Whatever do you mean, Arden dear?" Blossom Hoffstetter had queried, her hands cradling the wicker basket which contained the deviled ham and egg sandwiches she had prepared for their roadside lunch.

"It's all trees. How can you walk if there isn't any room to stand? How can you ever get to the top?"

"You needn't worry your sweet little head about reaching the top," she replied with a heart-warming smile, one that did justice to mothers everywhere across this great land. "Leave that to more adventurous sorts."

Years later he came to understand the mountain principle and he applied this self-realization to his own life. No one can tell you how to climb a mountain, he thought. You just have to get off your butt and do it for yourself.

There were other questions, other unexplained mysteries which haunted the waking hours of this wholesome clear-headed youth. But no longer did he turn to his parents for solutions to these puzzles. Instead, he pursued his own vast inner resources and, with the aid of the town library, more often than not found suitable answers.

Often, biographers, and chroniclers of other people's lives dig into the maze of youthful experience to draw forth analogies and ominous foreshadowings as to the effects these childhood occurrences made on the future adult. It is an intellectual game that usually becomes an exercise in false and pretentious scholasticism. But sometimes these writers, lacking as it were all manner of selfish and egotistical drive, come near to hitting the mark in their vicarious quest for immortality. Therefore:

For your reference files and with malice toward some, we give you Arden K. Hoffstetter, aged ten years and but a few months.

This town—his birthplace, this *shtetl* of overt

complacency was, twenty years ago, unmarred by ethnic or political crosscurrents. It was a large village of harmony, a portrait of American life that had been drawn with reasonable accuracy by Sinclair Lewis, Thomas Wolfe, and later by Grace Metalious. It was a small moment of paradise, a featurette Camelot to those who lived here, to those whose fathers and foremothers had journeyed with pioneer spirit and buckshot muskets to kill the heathen Indian, build their houses, and reap their modest Calvinist fortunes. Such was their treasured heritage and they were happy, content to see that little was changed. The God-head continued to shower the citizenry with undiminished and frequent bursts of divine light. There was an honor roll for the men and boys who had given their lives in two world wars, stalwart youths who had fought to make this town safe for normalcy. The Bijou maintained a policy of changing its feature every second Wednesday of the month There were no censorship problems; if a movie was cut or a book removed from the library shelves, the deletions were never missed. Scandals were kept to the whispered confines of twilight rocking-chair porches where fireflies darted through acacia-shrouded dusks and fine embroidered curtains stirred with each gently scented zephyr. But in one such house, a place we have visited briefly on Elm Street, future fomentation lurked inside the mind of a tall-for-his-age and baffled little boy.

For months the question, the problem, had plagued him. His fudge-making mother, his pipe-smoking father, could not be relied upon for answers or specific nuggets of information. What happened, where did it go? he wanted to know. After the dangling chain with its carved wooden handle was pulled with a jerk, the sound rattled the walls; the liquid swirled and the overhead tank filled once again with water. After everything he deposited had gone, had disappeared in a bubbly whirlpool flash, where was the refuse carried?

Sanitation and God, the virtues of clean living: these

ideas, these unwritten formulas had been drummed into him for years. Yet no explanations were given, no careful interpretations forthcoming. He would have to discover the true nature of these disembodied practices all by himself.

Arden left the bathroom after washing his hands, stood silently at the top of the landing and listened to the laughter of Uncle Miltie coming from the recently purchased Andrea television set, then turned and crept up the stairs to the attic. He lifted the trap door and stuck his head into the musty, cobwebbed room. Faint scurryings of things his mother baited with dry cheese, and he saw the light of a waning moon filtering through the one dusty window. In the shadows he made out the figure of his once-beloved rocking horse, an old chest of drawers with the walnut veneer splintering off the sides, the console radio that his father had huffed and puffed all the way from the living room. His eyes searched the corners, slid across the sloping unplastered ceiling. A deserted hornets' nest dating from three biteful summers back still clung to one of the beams. But he wasn't satisfied. There was no tank, no tub for collection of things that were considered unmentionable, things that could not be brought up at dinner, things that were euphemized, material objects that he would write about twenty years from now much to the distaste of some public defenders of virtue who would call his prose "sick, shameful, and in excruciatingly bad taste."

"Where did it go? The question, this ponderous weight of the unknown, jarred within him. If not hidden somewhere in the attic, perhaps the answer could be found at the opposite end. Perhaps he had approached the problem backwards.

He hurried downstairs, lurched past the dark parlor and the blue glow of tobacco smoke and video tubes and found the light switch which flooded the basement with harsh electric clarity.

Jars of plum and crab-apple preserves down in this

cool damp larder. Rusty garden tools and a broken ironing board, wooden-slatted summer deck chairs gathering dust and mildew. A tricycle without a front wheel leaning precariously against a pile of cardboard boxes labeled in his mother's flowery handwriting: LIFE, THE SAT. EVEN. POST, COLLS.

At a moment when acute disappointment seemed to take hold, his roving eyes caught sight of the damp glint of metal. He walked across the concrete floor, reached up and tentatively grabbed hold of one of the plumbing fixtures, a thick metal tube which fanned out above his head. His hand came away moist and cold. Nearby he detected a pipe bearing heat. He followed their passage, observed where they entered a hole in the ceiling and disappeared upstairs.

The running water! and he began to understand the dynamics of living, of day-to-day survival.

He walked farther, and in the darkest corner of the cellar a black lead pipe, another antiquated reminder of when this structure had first been built, shoved itself into the foundations of the house, reaching into the very bowels of the earth.

"Whatever are you doing down there, Arden?" his mother asked, appearing as a silhouette at the top of the stairs.

"Exploring," he said weakly.

"Don't you go rummaging through the magazines, you hear. That's not for little fellers. Why don't you come up and have some fudge? I saved the bowl for you to lick."

The idea was tempting. He turned to go and thought he heard a fly buzzing around the pipe in the corner. Then his mother came halfway down.

She warned, "Don't you go near there."

"Why not?"

"How'd you like to fall in? Then you'd really be sorry."

"What is it?" noticing for the first time another trap door, not unlike the one which led to the attic.

"Do I have to spell it out for you? That's the cesspool. Just come on up here this instant. Don't dally Arden. This instant!"

Sitting in the kitchen, a large glass of milk and a piece of fudge in front of him, Arden was temporarily satisfied. He had uncovered the mystery and felt that, under the circumstances, Frank and Joe Hardy could not have done much better. He now knew where all the dirty whispered-about things went after he pulled the chain. For the moment, he concentrated on the hungry rumbles of his stomach.

This experience, however innocuous and lacking in all manner of originality, was, nevertheless, the spawning ground and germinal point for Hoffstetter's future epic: *Flush*, a huge sprawling novel of urban civilization, a novel which traced the development of modern sewage disposal and the men who made that dream come true, a work he hoped would bring him the kudos of the tastemakers and those in the know. Indeed, it was a novel he liked to think of as destined to appeal to the scatological and coprophilic conscience of America.

"They scare you when there's three together like that," Arden heard a woman who trembled say to her friend. He turned his head around and watched three young Negro boys walk down the street.

They were walking up 86th Street in the direction of the subway. Belinda was swinging her hips from side to side, a portrait of obvious abandon and careless indecisive rhythm.

"I'm sorry if I was cross," she burst out in a rare display of good humor. "I'm just very intense these days."

"So I've gathered. But you needn't worry. I'm not one to hold grudges," linking his hand in hers. "In fact, it's almost a pleasure to see someone acting honestly these days."

"Meaning?"

"Meaning that everyone conducts himself as if he was playing a role, as if he's constantly on stage before a mass audience. And the more people act, the more they carry on, the less kind they become. Very few, it seems, are able to look objectively at their own shortcomings. But you can."

"And what *are* my shortcomings, if I may be so bold as to ask?"

Whether she was annoyed or just standing up for her rights, Arden K. couldn't tell. But since this was a free country, or thought it was, he went on, "You know what I mean, dear. It's just that the more people I come in contact with, the more aware I become that there aren't too many of us out there who even like who we are. But you seem to relish your identity, thrive on it so to speak, and I find that quite charming and wonderfully refreshing."

"You *are* a dear," she affirmed what his mother had always told him with a gentle squeeze of her fingers. "And just for that display of confidence I'm going to be totally me this afternoon. That is, if you'll only trust me."

"Of course I will," still giddy from her compliments.

"No, I'm serious. Trust me today. Even if tomorrow you hate me, today just believe in what I do." She was quite serious now. "For today, if all goes well, you'll get to see the real unadulterated Belinda as no one else has."

Arden was not completely sure of what she was driving at, but the prospect intrigued him and he tossed out a knowing paper smile.

At the corner of Third Avenue, opposite a papaya juice stand—"Nature's own energizer"—Hoffstetter's attention was drawn to the window of a narrow little shop specializing in magic-trick supplies, tourist mementos made in Japan, and other assorted novelties. He dragged Belinda along with him, stuck his nose against the glass and studied the odd jumble within. At the bottom of the display case he counted seven dead house flies with their

53

legs in the air, obvious victims of last summer's heat spell and the store's disregard for the therapeutic sinus-drying comforts of air-conditioning. There were plastic ice cubes with plastic roaches inside, whoopee cushions that traded on the lay public's weakness (or passion) for devices which faithfully imitated flatulent noises, as well as miniature replicas of the Empire State Building, Harlem, and the Statue of Liberty—obvious choices for the discerning consumer. Arden drummed his finger on the glass.

"See that?" pointing to an upper and prominent display stand.

Belinda squinted because the sun's reflection coming through the window made it difficult to see. "I'm trying."

An expression of joy shone on Arden K.'s face and he had trouble maintaining his composure. "That, my dear," shaking more than slightly, "is why my novel is going to grab hold of the public eye and never let go. For five years I've held forth on my beliefs, even while others tried to condemn me," although he could not think of one Other who had said anything to stand in his way. He rapped his wildly gesticulating finger on the window with even greater force. "That, Belinda my flower, is the essence of this country, the very distillation of American culture." There were strains of a loud self-proclaimed triumph in his voice.

"What?" and she screwed up her brows according to preconceived notions of quizzical expression, her lips forming an explanation point between two highly colored cheeks.

The words caught in his throat, sticky with Scotch-taped emotion. "Plastic cow pies. Rubber cow flops. Celluloid mounds of reproduced vomit hand-painted in three vivid lifelike colors. Honest-to-God artificial dog turds. You name the stool and they've got it. If not, they'll probably make it up to order. That's what this store sells and that's what keeps the business going. 'Amuse your friends. Startle your relatives. Be the hit of the party. Looks like the real thing. Almost feels like it too!' say the labels. But this is what America wants, what it thinks it needs and what it really hungers after!"

"You're out of your head, you know that," she turned on him with a scowl that was half fright and half indignation.

"Not at all! Not at all! There's a market for machine-made imitations of things that only living creatures can manufacture. It goes all the way back to organic chemistry and the synthesis of urea. Don't you see what everyone's been concentrating on? As if our whole culture, our entire western civilization, is striving toward that final moment of pure Hegelian synthesis. Don't you see the flash of cosmic unity? Doesn't everything finally fall into place?"

"No!" she exploded.

"But you will. I promise you that. Someday, you'll see, we'll all be able to buy lucite orgasms to have and hold, to cherish and fondle for our very own. Yep, the market's ripe for a novel like mine. Just you wait and see because I won't be around to say 'I told you so.'"

Belinda, surprisingly speechless and not equipped with a suitable comeback, urged him away from the window, pleading, "Arden, please. You'll be late for our appointment."

An unhealthy gleam emanated from his eyes. "Who cares about prior commitments! What matters is today and the here and now."

But when the light changed, his expression altered accordingly, from hot red to cool green. Dazed, he asked her, "I hope I didn't get too carried away. Sometimes I fear that I talk like a character I'm in the midst of creating. I wonder if what I have to say isn't really fictional prose instead of human speech."

"You're just too emotional," she chided him. "Be more gentle with yourself, Arden. Stop asking so many questions from life. Everything comes in time and with due process." But even she did not trust the echo of sincerity in her words. Were fame and the quest for the glory of the bitch goddess' Grail not a constant accumulation of impatient and exhausted moments, moments such as the one just past? Was there not danger, she wondered, imminent and terrible terrifying danger in letting go of one's ambitions for even just an instant?

Perhaps he's a genius after all, Belinda said to herself. Maybe I've taken him for granted all these months. Maybe I'm being unkind by not wanting to listen, by luring him into paths that could prove to be his ruin. Who knows, he just might be preaching the true gospel and morality of tomorrow, and there's no reason why I can't use my friendship with him to get right in the picture and get what I want.

For a second she visualized herself in the role of a white-robed Earth Mother, a near-Virgin demi-moral, a prophetess of the Second Coming who never left the side of this new messiah. History had shown her the basic and inherent validity of her hopes and aspirations. If Christ could have gotten as far as he did, despite the fact that he had a Jewish mother, why couldn't she?

"Wasn't Mary responsible for the whole thing, anyway?" she whispered to herself. "*Nudjehing* him constantly, saying, 'What are you doing with this filthy business? Sawdust and shavings. Your hands full of splinters. Who needs it? Better you should be a rabbit than a carpenter. Carpentry's for the *goyim*; it's just not a trade for Jewish boys.'"

Angels in transparent silk hummed a fetching tune by Jerry Herman and there in the heavens, rising in a stately mandala with a body by Fisher, she saw Sister Belinda shining in all her deified glory.

They walked on, awed with their separate visions, until they came to the entrance to the subway. A small crowd of curious and enthralled pedestrians had gathered here to watch a fashion photographer taking pictures of his model. A dark-haired boy with a Hasselblad camera in his hand, his neck festooned and weighed down by a trio by Leica, Nikon, and Minolta—ridiculous choices for the true professional—shouted in a clipped Etonian accent; "Move your hand to the right. Turn left. Show those pearlies, baby! Fabulous. Now right. That's perfect. Swing around. Good, good. Beautiful. I think we'll print it." His hair flew in his eyes and absently he brushed it aside. The comments were directed at the model, a lithe young man with a narrow waist and a thick crop of curling sun-bleached hair.

Suede vests and fur jackets were removed and tossed on the sidewalk where a woman snatched them up admiringly, blowing on the fur, fingering the leather, and telling her friend, "Feel that pelt. Look at those skins. What workmanship! Did you ever see anything so gorgeous in all your life? You can tell they didn't buy it wholesale!"

As for the fashion figures, they were kept busy as a variety of poses were held then discarded. The crowd watched with hushed and rapturous attention.

Arden felt that he could hear each one thinking, "This is a moment I'll have to tell my grandchildren about!"

"When they comin' out? What magazine?" the lady insisted on knowing. "Isn't it just too thrilling!" she exclaimed when she saw she had aroused Hoffstetter's interest. "The world of high fashion is so exciting, so dynamic and versatile, don't you agree?" A look of rare pride encapsulated her wrinkled features.

"New location!" the photographer shouted, tossing the strap of the camera over his neck. "Brownstones. Gotta find a batch of town houses." He began to gather up his costly equipment as the other boy flung the items of clothing and current style over his arm. The bystanders moved off in all directions, dazed and mumbling catchy phrases of utter contentment, and Arden, a stickler for details, tapped the dark-haired young man on the shoulder, asking,

"Excuse me, but I was wondering what kind of film you were using. I'm sort of an amateur buff myself," shuffling his feet awkwardly from side to side as he was apt to do in the presence of those in the arts.

The camera-wearer, uncapped lenses jostling each other in the hollow of his chest, looked to see if he was still being watched. "Who uses film," he said at last, at which point Arden's eyebrows jumped up along his forehead.

"But I thought you were taking pictures for one of the magazines."

"Listen friend, we're just waiting to be discovered."

"By whom?"

The young man put his hands on his hips and spread his legs slightly. "You must be kidding," he decided. "I mean, are you for real or aren't you? I mean, who's putting on who?"

Arden fidgeted uncomfortably, aware of the camera-wearer's insistent gaze.

"Lookit, the only problem about living in New York is that it has decided disadvantages. Like there isn't any place in town comparable to Schwab's drugstore. If you want to break into pictures..."

"Oh, the movies!" Arden said with relief. He had been thinking of British perversions, Spanish *putos*, catamites, and the tortured streets of Marrakech, but now he relaxed.

"Of course! But if you want to make it to the screen you either have to be a waiter at Sanctuary—now that Arthur's closed—or sell Aramis at Bonwit's for Esteé. There's no room for beautiful wholesome boys anymore," he concluded with disgust and a set of crow's-feet that told Arden the search had been going on for quite some time.

Arden K. felt a pang of sympathy for their plight,

despite their advancing years. He looked warmly from one boy to the other. "We're on our way out to Brooklyn to see Bernie Guysman. . . ."

"Brooklyn!" the two of them said with abhorrent amazement and Hoffstetter turned his head around to see if he had made a *faux pas*, expecting to find it lying desolately on the sidewalk.

"I used to live in the Heights," volunteered the more lightly complexioned fellow in a see-through shirt. "But I had to get away before it blew my mind. There are so many sick people living over there, out on the streets at every hour of the day."

"Bernie Guysman!" said the cameraman, not having gotten over Arden's disclosure. "That faker! That horse thief! Raoul," motioning to his friend, "and I used to work as a team for that phony. Let me tell you, you can't make a penny in dirty movies. It's just a real dead-end, dog-eat-dog, back-against-the-wall business. I should know and I'd be the last person in the world to steer you wrong."

"But they're not dirty anymore," Arden replied, wondering why he was taking the defense of a man he hadn't even met. "They're experimental and *avant-garde*."

"Someone's been giving you the old snow job, that's for sure," the youth said with a smile.

"Besides," Raoul spoke up. "There just doesn't seem to be any room these days for a beautiful face," striking a favorable pose on his good side. "I've been seriously considering scarring myself. It might give my obviously strong Celtic features a fresh kind of tough chic. Anyway, everything imperfect and ugly is so in, you know. I mean, that's how commercial the industry's gotten."

"Well," Arden said, feeling the tug of Belinda's hand at his sleeve, "I'm sorry I can't be of any more help. Good luck and I hope you and your classic features get found."

"By and by," Raoul assured him.

"Everyone gets found sooner or later," said his friend. "You just have to be in the right place at the right time."

Then Arden K. and Belinda descended the subway steps as their shoes squashed empty gum wrappers and discarded cigarette packs—the nation trying desperately to give up the habit. They moved down the smooth poured-concrete steps which led into the bowels of Big City, unknowingly intent upon discovering their selves.

Chapter 2½

THE AUTHOR wishes to acknowledge his appreciation and gratitude to R. Wreid and *American Dramaturgy* for permission to reprint the following article.

THE BRANCH BLUES OR
MAIN STREET DISINTERRED

Reality. That's what he's selling in *Flush*. And everyone's buying.

Up on the twenty-seventh floor of the Henry Hudson Hotel, in a suite best described as American incinerator, the tall swaying figure of Wisconsin's Wonderkid, Arden K. Hoffstetter, stalks across the unwaxed floor like a hyena who has suddenly lost his laugh. Seriousness rolls up along his forehead like breaking waves as he whirls deftly around and says with deadpan incisiveness, "Fame, I've decided, is a trap for small-town egos. What I want now is simply power!" Then he breaks into a chuckle that's been overhauled and unspoiled by years of inattention. But success ain't getting to his head, even though, baby—they're all paying attention like it's going out of style!

It's the often-heard story of the struggling writer who made good, only this writer is no Jacqueline Susann. Either he's loved or he's hated, but no one puts down Hoffstetter with a toss and a shrug. The big boys in the galleys game over at Bennett Cerf's house of printed

61

profits call him the hottest property to come their way since Philip Roth shocked a nation with *Portnoy's Complaint*. Warner Brothers predicts that the movie version alone (with Hoffstetter getting top billing) will gross upward of eight figures.

Looking at him at first glance, he reminds you of Holden Caulfield grown up, with a narrow J. D. Salinger horsey face and a pair of wildly gesticulating hands. His mouth has as much expression as a wet cornflake, but when he starts to say something you stop and listen with jaws agape to the snap, crackle, and pop of his rare articulation.

Moving deftly through the hungry-eyed smash of autograph seekers and security guards stomping around the linoleum lobby, up in the bland-as-a-raw-mushroom cage of an elevator, his literary agent gurgles, "He's not looking for kind words, mind you," and, nervously fixing his four-in-hand knot, "You're a fortunate fellow; he really sympathizes with the free-lance crowd." Then into a room where lavender smoke lies in a muggy blanket suspended below the chipped plaster ceiling, where the wonder child himself sits dejectedly at the edge of an unmade bed, clusters of flowers strewn at his feet.

"I'm a freak for asphodels," he says morosely. "But it's been an unnerving morning. Absolute madness!"

The agent looks like Eugene McCarthy strained through a bedpan, with the same kind of starved poet's eyes. He snatches a cigarette out of his Harris-tweed pocket and his hands shake as he draws a light. "Why didn't you say something? Let me know, at least."

Hoffstetter looks mildly surprised, then turns to me. "He made me," pointing to the lanky silver-haired S.A.R. man. "Without his help I'd never even have gotten my feet wet. If he hadn't recognized my talent I'd still be reading the slush pile for every other publishing house in the city. Thanks, baby," and he motions him out with a friendly but forceful wave of his hand.

"He has other clients. God knows I take up too much of his time already," Hoffstetter says after the door closes, slouching like a puppet with its strings released. He lets his gaze linger on the syrupy ocher walls where sunmotes crawl off like stuck flies, then he looks intensely with a set of coming-on-strong eyes, cocking his head to one side, asking, "What do you think? Do you think I have what it takes?"

"Who's to say?" I reply weakly.

"That's what I like," reaching over to thump me on the back. "Creative honesty. Honestly, it's like the American dream come true." He gets to his feet, shuffles over to the window, and draws apart the slats of the venetian blind. He stands there silently, then gives a quick famished look over his shoulder. "See that city?" He taps against the unwashed glass. "I've tried to capture the sounds of its people. I've given five years of my life to this town. Five years of dedication. Two thousand days of sitting up nights till my neck felt like a dry twig ready to snap right off. Why shouldn't I be proud. I went through seventeen typewriter ribbons getting the book finished. But I'm frightened, really godawfully scared right down to my roots. Next month I go out to the Coast to start the movie. You know, just the interiors. The rest they'll shoot back here. Would you believe, *me* in the movies! And to think some jealous sonuvabitch once said my voice was too nasal." He pounds his chest and struggles with a rasping laugh. "But that's what I want. Total control over the media. *I* think the ideas. *I* write the words. *I* do the scenario and *I* play the character. And you know what?" as he comes back across the room, "They're all waiting for me to fall on my face. No, I mean it. No one likes nothing more than a fallen superstar. Only, you know what? It's not gonna happen, baby. Belinda taught me all about setbacks and they're no longer part of my lingo." He shuts his eyes with exhaustion.

Before we had agreed on the interview, the first that he

has ever given, I had made a rather feeble attempt at getting another angle, another viewpoint as to the Hoffstetter personality. One of his oldest and closest friends is Broadway actress Belinda Blumright, a loud and brassy charmer, a natural zany who's already clawed her way to the lead in a new Merrick musical. "It's like this," she said over a dish of yogurt at the Colony. "Arden K.'s still a child. He still hasn't found himself. He likes to think he's the new Renaissance-type man, only he's deathly afraid of being put down or called a mere dabbler, a dilettante. Absolute perfection has become an obsession with him. People like Arden, no matter how many awards they achieve, just never find happiness."

Maybe so, but when he's not working, not pecking furiously at his battered Underwood portable, Hoffstetter is as full of wit and flamboyant guile as the best of us. "My biggest hassle is not knowing how to relax," he admits. For "Come ball with me" seems to be his motto and a whole new generation has discovered in his writing that the things that go on behind locked doors aren't necessarily dirty. His style, referred to by some as "Dynamic Eclecticism or Early Sincere," is a combination of nothing else you've ever read. What makes *Flush* doubly exciting is the wide range of its appeal, the basic underlying readability of its prose and, yet, the vivid power and force it creates and keeps on generating. Unlike most things being published these days, this epic novel doesn't get soft in the middle.

Someone phones and he picks up the receiver, blurting out after a few moments, "Tacky! Tacky! Who do you take me for, anyway?" He slams down on his connection, genuinely angry. "Some freak wants me to do a deodorant commercial. That's what Belinda likes to call *chutzpah!*"

He lies down on the bed with the crumpled chenille spread, still mumbling about spraying hexachlorophene and aluminum chlorhydroxide under his arms, blows smoke rings into the air as my tape recorder whirls on.

"It's lost forever," he moans. "The innocence of watching Dinah Shore, Beulah, and Perry Como. America's changing hands, changing heads, and no one bothers to wash before meals.

"Wreid, when I was a kid, still in high school, I got the faculty adviser of the drama society to let me put on my own play. I thought I had novel, even revolutionary ideas about what constituted good theater, so we rehearsed using one script that read like a town pageant, while on the sly I greased a few palms and paid off the students who dreamed of conquering Shubert Alley. Had them memorize lines for an altogether different dramatic experience. I bet you're wondering why I'm bringing this up, but I just want to show you that I've been an innovator for more years than it took writing *Flush*.

"The play was tentatively entitled *The Branch Blues*, Branch being the name of our high school. It was a one-shot-performance deal with all the proceeds going to the football team for new uniforms and we sold out every seat in the auditorium. The night we were scheduled to go on I slipped some additional encouragement into every participating kid's hand, right down to the lighting crew. When the curtain went up, with the mayor and his wife and all the town aldermen with their wives sitting so primly and self-righteously in the front row, boy were they in for a surprise." At which point he props himself up on his elbow and looks intently at the reel of tape going around in slow circles. Satisfied, the author yawns, smiles and goes on, "A trumpet blares a marvelous fanfare and out step six naked baton twirlers singing 'Columbia the Gem of the Ocean' with background music by Charles Ives. You should have heard the audience roar. But they wouldn't let it go on—even though the next scene was going to be a stroke of real brilliance—and about half a dozen apoplectic mothers wearing stone martens with little stuffed heads and nasty clawed paws come tear-assing behind the curtain, screaming for their daughters' collective loss of chastity. How I ever got out of that unholy business is another story altogether, but it just goes to show you that my head wasn't always in the clouds. I mean, honestly, my dreams were always grounded on actual fact. If they weren't, I wouldn't be anywhere today and that's no lie."

Hoffstetter pats his stomach. "You want something to eat?" and gets on the house phone and orders up a couple of liverwurst sandwiches. "No mayo," he says with dignified and seasoned aplomb, giggling slyly. "Sorry I didn't reserve the Orange Room at Nedick's." Then he seems to remember something and says, "In fact, one of my dreams used to be just this, having you, R. Wreid, interviewer of the stars, do a piece on me." He leans forward and winks conspiratorially. "Someday I'll do an interview on you, feller," he says with a smile as a toilet flushes across the hall and I get up to stretch my legs.

But *someday* for Arden K. Hoffstetter is nowhere in the near future. At the rate he's going, he's liable to turn American culture completely inside out.

And baby, that's no lie.

Chapter 3

"Trust me."

"I can't, not when I'm afraid of labyrinths."

"Belinda sweetheart, it's all very simple. We take the express to Utica Avenue. ..."

"Where's that?" and her eyes look like saucers from a doll-house collection.

"In Brooklyn," he replies patiently.

"I know that. But where in Brooklyn?"

"I told you. In Brownsville."

"Is that a good section? I thought Brooklyn was all a slum."

"Not at all, dear. Leave everything to me. We take the express to Utica, then switch over to the local for just one stop." Arden explains after they have purchased tokens and passed through the turnstile onto the rank-and-file-smelling platform.

"Filth City, indeed!" she declares, her nostrils revolted at every turn. Then she asks him, "How long?" For questions are far easier for her to master than factual statements embodying ideas and programs for daily living.

"Maybe forty minutes," thinking of many people (in past moments and situations similar to this) who have told him that his patience is virtuous and how what a wonderful teacher he'd make. "A little more or a little less. He said he'd be at the studio all afternoon, so I could come at my convenience."

"That's very white of him," she smirks, returning to her usual demeanor. "Big shots don't usually find time to chat with strangers."

Arden looks surprised. "But he's not. Not really. A friend of a friend of mine is his secretary and Girl Friday. She arranged the whole thing. Anyway, unknown writers are always much kinder in print. He told me himself that he's tired of being knocked down by every establishment magazine in town."

She puts her hand on her hip and cocks her knee, promoting the illusion (in his mind) that she is preparing to kick him according to ways and means outlined on wrestling cards. "Which means, if I may be so outgoing, that you are intending to sell out by not writing the truth as you really see it." The knee wobbles, vagaries of old athletic girl gymnast accidents, and she pushes it back into place by slapping her patella with the palm of her hand.

"Not so. You forget," Arden reminds her, "that Guysman's not paying me to do the piece. He won't even ask to see the first draft. All he wants is someone who will give the whole thing a fresh approach. If it works out, and I do a good enough job, chances are the article might be bought by *Evergreen* or even *Screw*. And the extra bit of bread and added exposure certainly won't hurt my career any."

"Career—hah! I've heard that one before, too," she snorts knowingly and with new-found malice, carrying over the melody of causticness into her next statement, "You have it all planned out, don't you my darling stud?"

Arden decides that she is what Shirley K. Peterson and others have called a "primary hostile" and that her goading is only a sign of latent immaturity, so he lets it pass, asking, "Want some gum?"

"It'll be stale." Belinda moves down the platform past narrow tiled niches which housed public telephones in the late thirties, to find a seat on one of a row of green contour chairs. Behind her a poster proclaims the critical praises heralding the coming of a new movie based on the life of Frank Harris. She turns her head around and reads the copy aloud, as if Arden is an illiterate in need of enlightenment. "'Makes the book look like Little Red Riding Hood,' says *Life* magazine. 'I loved every minute of this new unexpurgated spectacular,' writes *Women's Wear Daily*. 'Dustin Hoffman's performance merits *two* Oscars, not one. This is going to be the year's Big One,' applauds the *Daily News* with ***½."

"Sounds good," he comments after she is finished.

"Sounds dreary. *Variety* says that he got the part just on the basis of the size of his equipment."

"Belinda!" and he is believably, if not altogether rightly, shocked.

"Get your mind out of the gutter," she sneers. "*Vocal* equipment. He's got a big box and a good set of chords. The part demands excessive moments of prolonged spasmodic grunting, groaning, and asthmatic wheezing. Honestly, Arden, sometimes you act like a child."

"Better to act like a child than look like a fool," at which point he shudders because he doesn't understand what he has just said and if there is anything that upsets Arden K., it is saying things independently of his own conscious thought processes.

When the train comes, Belinda holds down her hair with both her hands, looking like a stick-up victim, because she does not like to use hair sprays, thinking they give the scalp an artificial and unhealthy sheen. The string of cars screeches to a jolting halt known to millions upon millions of human beings either through actual experience or the benefit of other media. When the doors open they find a seat in the half-filled car, for Big City underground trains do not fill up until people get tired and want to go home to the six o'clock news. The travelers who have been jostled at every station along the line for the past forty-five minutes and who are now only perhaps a little more than halfway to their ultimate destinations give Arden K. and Belinda a few sets of suspicious and alienated-looking stares—chartreuse jersey and chocolate-brown velvet considered a shade too subversive—venereal glances of unabashed hostility, and the unfound talented pair cringe with shrinking necks, hunching and shrugging them like collapsing turtling telescopes into their shoulders. Arden is sorry he hasn't bought himself a piece of penny machine gum, for chewing tends—as the copywriters declare—to rid the thoughts of unwarranted belligerence, while at the same time admirably stretching one's coffee break. When the doors close on someone's leather handbag which is soon enough wrenched free with a broken strap, the train starts up again and the lights go out. Arden shuts his eyes and does something unbeknownst to the other passengers, even to the girl who sits by his side making plans of her own.

He ruminated. The milch of daydreams—an agelong and habitual preoccupation—took hold of his unconsciousness and eyes drooping with sudden fatigue and oddly flattened lids, Arden escaped into a sphere, a realm of disquieting and disturbing remembrances. To show how tricky the mind can be, just before he had stepped onto the subway car his eyes had passed over a sign he had unknowingly committed to memory, an embossed metal plaque which announced, "Obstructions and other such violations will be fully persecuted by law."

Now his mindwaves flutter and turn with tropistic energy to his mother's sister and he is somewhere in his budding pubescent years, listening to his parent (for his father has since been buried without pomp or circumstance) explain over a dinner plate of Yankee pot roast, "I'm afraid that your Aunt Violet may be reaching the end of her appointed time on this good earth. I know it's not table talk, Arden dear, but the poor woman has been constipated for the last seven days. A week is not something to smile over and I fear the worst."

He looks up, dangling brown meat at the end of his fork.

"I fear," she goes on dramatically, "that she has an obstruction." She chokes on her food, although there is nothing in her mouth, wipes her lips with a corner of her napkin and swallows water.

Arden has never heard that word used with such odious connotations. He asks his mother, careful to chew and swallow his food before talking, "Has she consulted the appropriate authorities?"

Blossom reaches across the table to affectionately stroke the crown of his head. "Such a way with words," she murmurs. "He gave her a shot of penicillin and some pills, large oblong things, she said. Could almost choke a horse, but she's still complaining of pains in her lower back. Do you think it might be the real thing?" Blossom Hoffstetter wants to know with an expression of utter dejection, complete and premature aggrievement.

"Perhaps." Being too good a son, considerate and trustworthy, he is not cruel enough to reveal to her his true suspicions, that Violet is suffering from the ravages of a gonococcal organism of unknown origin. His extensive studies of natural and industrial effluents have led him to this uncompromising, if somewhat incredible, conclusion. But he buttons his lip and stares down at the yellow washes of creamed corn which stream across his plate.

"An obstruction," his mother sighs again, only this time even louder than before, convinced that the end is just around the corner. "Who would have suspected? Who would have thought it could happen to my side of the family? We all have such long life spans." And a scant tear or two falls from her eyes.

Arden gets up and leans over his mother, patting her hand and touching his lips to her cheek. "Don't cry, mother. We've all done the best we can." But at the same time he feels guilty, knowing that he has sorely neglected consanguineous duties by failing to call Violet at her Wauwatosa villa and relay a few words of condolence.

An obstruction, he thinks, and now they'll have to operate and then she'll wither away with inoperable speed and her friends will soon enough stand at graveside, life's-end, whimpering softly, but loud enough to be heard, into starched lace hankies, "I just saw her the other day. She looked so healthy, played such a splendid game of bridge. Only forty-nine and such a young woman, still in her prime!"

But, miraculously, the floodgates are lowered and two days later, Blossom already making preparations to have her black crepe taken out of storage and freshly cleaned according to current French processes, her sister calls to inform her that everything is back to normal. The obstruction, that bolus of malignant worry, is no longer there. Everything is unhampered. "It just might have been a hairball," Violet consoles her younger sister, and Arden's mother remembers that in Wauwatosa, Violet keeps a houseful of seven Burmese cats, all with evil yellow eyes.

"Do be more careful and hygienic, Violet love. Such calamities are ill-advised, you know. We don't want a recurrence of what Papa would have called 'a nasty business,' now do we." As Violet has called collect and before six with the good news, Blossom draws the conversation to a close. "And do let me hear from you. And don't forget that your baby sister still worries her heart out." The last is said in a shout, as if she fears that the dying connection, this last valedictory link, might foreshadow more disastrous events to come.

Carcinoma was the name of the game, Arden recalls, returning to wakefulness. And the Hoffstetters played to win.

"Did I tell you that I went to the opera?" Belinda asks as the train slides into the Fifty-ninth Street groovy station where Bloomingdale's and Alexander's have both leased space to display their merchandise and where there is a free transfer between the BMT and the IRT, should you ever feel the need to change connections.

"Tell me," he encourages her, painting a patient tutorial and listening face.

"It was a benefit performance...."

"For whom?"

"Does it matter?"

"It does for me. If I don't know who the benefit was for, how can I even begin to benefit from your telling?"

"I saved the program. You can look at it later. God," tossing her unlacquered hair with exasperation, "You *are* an inquisitive one."

"You needn't get stuffy about it," feeling the need for an honest repartee.

"Arden, will you please let me go on and stop begrudging me a bit of limelight!"

"Go on."

"Thank you." She folds her hands in her lap, waits for the doors to close again and tells him, "It was a performance of *Turandot*—you know, the opera made famous by that prep-school writer—directed by Tom O'Horgan. Remember him? The guy who staged *Hair* a couple of seasons ago. Actually, it was quite brilliant, if a little chaotic, although they could have picked better bodies."

"Isn't opera more concerned with vocal abilities rather than physical accoutrements?"

"Physiques, you mean? I suppose," she agrees. "But when you're seeing a performance done in the nude, it's nice to have something pretty to look at. What did work though, was that the traditional barriers between audience and performers were totally broken down. You might just as well have been sitting in their bathrooms, listening to them singing as they took their morning shower, you felt so close."

"I was under the impression that these barriers you speak of were knocked aside and thrown down several seasons ago," he says knowingly with a twist of his lips.

"So they were," holding back her desire to slap him in the teeth, thinking, Let him talk about novels and books. When it comes to the world of theater, that's my sacred precinct. He should know better than to cross a starstruck child of fortune.

"But not at the Met, *darling*," she says, clenching her too-perfect teeth, shining white caps ready to impress the buyers. "You should have seen the bedazzled Gucci-Pucci crowd stamping their feet and yelling out bravos. And when Birgit Nilsson—trooper that she is—sang 'In Questa Reggia,' I thought that the ceiling would come down on everyone's head. Everybody just went mad."

He replies succinctly, "I prefer 'Nessun Dorma,' myself."

Belinda looks surprised. "I didn't know you followed opera."

"I've been reading *books*, my dear, not only writing them." Arden nods his head in an approximation of Blumright conceit, deciding that it is time the girl took some of her own medicine. "And how was Corelli?"

Right after this remark, Belinda seems to lose her composure. "Cute as a panda," she tells him, suddenly withdrawn and defensive. "Why don't we talk about something else?"

"All right."

But they were both silent, moving apart so that a few inches of seat show between their rounded thighs and curving buttocks. But at Fourteenth Street, a bag breaks and the two of them are jerked to communicating response, mutual attention.

It happened so fast, so quickly, that Arden—usually prepared and almost waiting for inevitabilities—would have been thrown from his place had Belinda not reached over and shielded the forward thrust of his body's astonishment with her outstretched arm. Considerate in times of emergencies, she already showed signs of maturing into a splendid performer. His chest heaved and pressed against the chartreuse jersey of her jumpsuit, so that the fabric threatened to give way to bare skin.

It seems that when the train slid into the station where an anonymous voice challenged the brave and disbelieving with cries of, "Stand clear of moving platforms as trains enter and leave the station," it did so without professional smoothness or concern for the comfort and safety of its passengers. This being the unfortunate case, a lady rider waiting by the sliding doors was thrown off balance so that her body wrapped itself around the aisle pole and her overloaded shopping bag slipped off her wrist and was dashed to the floor. Out tumbled and rolled down the busy-footed aisle: cans and plastic bottles, containers and aerosol dispensers. The woman, nondescript if not for her faintly pink marcelled hair (which Arden found clever, if not in particularly good taste), screamed behind her pale parched, almost waxen, lips and ran frantically—as women do in search of bargains— after her scattered possessions. Some watched the hot pursuit with bland disinterest; others were more outspoken and curiously moved to clicking their tongues against their hard palates, making sounds which when put in print resembled a succession of sharply accented *Tsks*. Otherwise, they said nothing, straining their eyes over the tops of their newspapers and paperback thrillers.

Picking up speed, she scooped up Ajax, Fantastik, and Cinch off the dirty foot-smeared floor, cracking and scratching her unpolished fingernails obviously unstrengthened with gelatin as she dug under the seats and between trouser- and stocking-shod legs to retrieve Handy Andy, Mr. Clean, and Comet. Lestoil joined Whistle and Favor; Bravo and Glory were tossed back into the shopping bag—miraculously intact—as the doors opened and an angry stampede of readers of the

Transit Times pushed past Top Job and Pledge, unmindful of the lady's dilemma.

"How dare you try to imitate the immaculate ways of the Muslim? You...you...cleaning freak!" shouts a natural Afro-processed, beret-donning Harlemite, kicking away a cylinder of Preen with the tip of his blucher-fitted foot.

The woman looks as if she is going or preparing either to have a heart attack or cry, maybe sit down or crumble onto the floor in general and agonizing despair, still jamming the purchases into her bag, forgetting that the doors are closing and she will undoubtedly miss her station, mumbling with harassed aggravation.

"But one wipes out dirt on contact and the other powers out stains. If it weren't for their concentrated bubbling action it wouldn't get the dirt that liquid cleaners leave behind. Besides, it gets out stains when other cleansers can't," she pleads with tired television eyes, pale and ghost-like, her voice falling to a pitiable drone, whispering as the cars sweep through the underground tunnels. "Like a white tornado. I saw the dove and the knight, the giant hand come right out of my washing machine. I saw it. Just like a white tornado...."

Arden K. closes his own eyes with grief and embarrassment, sees through his unblackened spotty mind flashing photo pictures and rotogravured impressions of (among others and other things) Jane Withers, Arthur Godfrey, Kaye Ballard, and Eddie Albert. He wants to sob, to sniffle rheumily for the woman who couldn't make up her mind, but he knows that if he interferes, if he gets off his seat and offers to help her find the last of the momentarily lost products, the other passengers would point and jeer. Belinda would probably not want to go on and she would turn away in a huff, get off at the next stop and take the uptown train back to Yorkville. (A place, it seems to him at this moment, where all things make sense, where all things must ultimately return.) So he keeps his blushing eyes closed and hopes that when he dares to open them again the lady will have gone into retirement and he can be left alone in peace.

"It takes all kinds," Belinda mutters her fondest cliché and Arden K. tends to agree, just on principle.

There was a word which had slipped his mind. It was used to measure the intensity of pollution of a body of water—a beach or a river or a sample from a kitchen tap. It had something to do with concentrations of certain microorganisms and particles of fecal matter, but five years ago, before Arden K. had written the first page or even a single word of *Flush*, such a need for infinite detail would not have troubled him. Five years ago he thought in more general terms, composing chalky outlines to broad areas of information, never seeing the need for *chiaroscuro*, for shadows and *quattrocento* highlighting, for penetrating *sfumatoe*ed exactitude.

He had come to Big City on a Greyhound bus a few weeks after graduating from college. He had been exempted from military service on the basis of his family composition: legally considered his mother's sole source of support, it was deemed unamerican (then) to separate widows from their only offspring. But Blossom had the qualities of a goldstar mother; filled with a rare kind of understanding, she even questioned his choice of transportation, telling him that there was quite enough money from his father's estate if he wanted to take a plane. Arden graciously refused. He had read many stories of people traveling East in search of fame and fortune and in every instance they had boarded a bus with their ticket clamped and clutched in their tight sweaty hand. So, at the time, he saw no need to deviate from what had already been established by those who had gone before. Besides, he was able to load on two large steamer trunks, thus saving himself the additional expense of overland shipping.

So he came; over the flat scenicless highways of Illinois, Indiana, and Ohio. Under the hollowed-out coal mountains of Pennsylvania, past the Hackensack marshes to the town where everything began and ended.

So he arrived.

And he underwent a subtle transformation, evolving from the small-town boy with urban ideas into the small-town young man now firmly entrenched in metropolitan culture. He found a room—more comfortable than he felt he was entitled to. He found friends, exciting personalities who taught him how to use the subways, how to borrow money, and how to buy on credit. He found work, jobs which became a series of mediocre paying and thoughtless exercises in mental tedium. Yet he was always content. He had his typewriter, his stack of paper, and for three years he lived the life he thought was relegated to all the Wolfes, Steinbecks, and Hemingways of the age. Then (some eight years before the *now* of our narrative) it was Uris and Wouk, Bellow maybe as well, who were out in front and winning, reaping, gleaning all the royalties. One heard from Jones and Mailer, young then and angry disenchanted voices who had no time away from their craft to seek a mayorality or rush about a nation with reportorial glee. It seemed as if everyone read and knew what it all meant, applying fictional lessons to their own uncertain lives.

So he struggled.

He pounded out a growing crescendo of typewritten pages, trying to immortalize the nebulous recollections of his youth and boyhood, attempting to impose upon his multitude of visions a Tolstoyan universality and closeness to the soil which he remembered as being part of his own early years: waking to the din of crows and falling asleep under roofs that hid star-spangled skies, passing into the world of dreams beneath frontier eiderdown to night sounds of crickets and owls. Yet the form eluded him. Lacking any feel for eurythmy, the words and phrases constantly drifted away without cohesion or power, without any sense of momentum or echo of impending doom.

There were moments when Arden K. felt himself edging toward disaster, failing and falling through lack of headway, tripping headlong into the snare, the pit that had captured hundreds of other aspiring talents. He saw the need for liberation, not confinement. Hoffstetter was a fighter, and he would not go the way of all those brilliant comparative lit majors who once had heard melodies redolent of divine calling, the sensual rustle of proof sheets and days of scratching out forbidden marginalia. No, he told himself in moments of despair, and these were many and of considerable duration. He would not turn away to lead the robot existence of a Madison Avenue caption writer, a jingle-maker, nor would he ever seek the role of editor, taking out his unrealized literary frustrations on every burgeoning eccentric talent that came his way. He would not fall back, fall behind or slip easily into line. He had to go on, to make it all work and see the goals—these self-wrought urgings—bear truthful fruit.

So he struggled anew.

He was loath to see Wallace and Robbins rediscovered a century after their deaths, to be extolled as the twin Charles Dickens of their age. Was there not a place in the annals of literary greatness and the pages of *Who's Who* for a Hoffstetter? he kept asking himself. Someone had told him that his first name implied trouble, that there was something unisexual about it. Now he began to look at himself as a Hesse figure reincarnated, an Arden-Ardena, a mental hermaphrodite of such recondite origins as to make Nabokov's serpentine prose look like simplicity itself. He had his fortune read:

... Sister Evada, spiritual reader & advisor will tell you what you want to know about friends, enemies, or rivals; how to gain the love you desire, control or influence the action of anyone even though miles away. Gives never-failing advice, reunites the separated and causes speedy, happy marriages. Overcomes enemies, evil habits, stumbling blocks and bad luck.

... This great lady guarantees to help you. She succeeds where others fail. *She is not false*. She has helped thousands & can help you too. She is the only one who can help you with problems such as love, courtship, marriage, divorce, business, lawsuits, etc.

... FIRST TIME IN THIS AREA.

... Lucky Charms given FREE with each reading, so be sure to come to the right address.

The aces, red and black, pile one upon the other, the cards predicting great success, but only by indicating at first a turning away, a removal from and denial of.

What? he asked himself.

One day he looked at the pile of neatly typed pages, proud of his sixty-five words-per-minute agility, but at the same time mortified tht he had wasted three years without once making sense, without giving the slightest breath of life to any of his characters—thinly masked (he saw then) representations of those in and out of authority who had made the rules and peopled his early years. Saddened as only artistic types can get after they indulge in a bout of self-laceration, moved not to tears but to immediate destruction, he began ripping the pages into manageable pieces, flushing them down the toilet with methodical and assertive speed. And then it hit him.

Why he had failed up to this point to see a new and vibrant image is another story altogether and is rather beyond the limited confines of this treatise. Let it suffice to say that Arden K.'s lifelong preoccupation with sewage disposal was paying off as now it all hit him like a torrent of suddenly released reservoir water. He knew that if he had been born a product of the Disney studio, a lightbulb would have flashed over his head, just as if he had been knocked unconscious, birds and stars would have been seen orbiting with halolike precision over the growing bump of his misfortunes. The sound of the toilet belching, gurgling into the sewer system of the greater metropolitan area, sent shivers of new and dazzling promise running down his back.

That day, a day five years ago, Arden K. Hofstetter sat down once again at his Underwood portable and wrote the first line of his as yet untitled mammoth fictional venture:

"The water was dotted with countless bloated upturned bellies of dead fish, a mass of putrefying organic matter that attracted gulls of three different and distinct types, including a solitary representative of the species *Larus minutus*—the little gull ('A rare straggler from Europe.')"

After this quasi-historical and altogether wonderfully romanic moment, the next five years were just an uphill slide.

She has nothing better to do, having not brought along a script or a book of plays to read on the way, so Belinda asks with uncommon demureness, "Tell me about your book. What's the story like? Is it dirty?"

The train is passing between Manhattan and Brooklyn. The string of lights flash on and off and the passengers engrossed in reading matter find themselves temporarily hard pressed. Arden replies, "If I could tell you about my book in three sentences, then I'd have had no business writing it." Immediately he feels cheap, although not necessarily guilty. He had heard another author make this same remark on a television show and he had subsequently incorporated it into the bulk of his compendium of witty sayings.

Unperturbed, the girl presses on in quest of new frontiers. "Is it about life?"

"Yes," he indulges her. "And about people. About feelings and events and trying times. All the stuff of latter-day classics."

"Do you think it'll sell?"

"You seem to have an intuitive grasp of what makes me miserable. I just hope it gets bought, my child. That's all that concerns me at the moment. I have no idea whether or not I'm writing for the mass market. An editor will have to make that distinction."

When Arden talks about his novel, his tongue tends to loosen and the range of his verbosity broadens proportionately. But he thinks that Belinda is only struggling with politeness, little knowing that she is trying to get on his good side while the going is still good, so that weary beyond his years or even his limited amount of recent rest, he shuts his eyes and concocts, orders precisely out of the stuff of dreams, a fantasy to entertain him as they travel beneath the unclean waters of the East River.

"And here he is, folks, the man you've all been waiting for. Here's Ar...den!" A burst of frenzied gunfire applause, the drumrolls of spontaneity, sending the hand-clapping meters off their scales and Hoffstetter pulls aside the curtain and beams at the camera eye. Millions and many more—single and in groups—watch in color and black-and-white within the privacy of their homes and castles and as he mounts to the slightly elevated conversation area, the spectators begin to exhibit patterns of berserk adoration. In the peanut gallery, a young girl sitting in the third row center begins to foam at the mouth, ripping her tartan plaid parochial-school pleated skirt into little pieces with her bare hands. The host, a replacement of the nation's current favorite and familiar face who is away on vacation, stands up from his Danish modern swingback chair and imitates the reaction of the studio audience. Arden looks bashful, masking his fully controlled feelings of animal pride and authority. Confidently and without overstepping his bounds, he shakes hands with the stand-in comic, kisses the cheek of the dumb-blonde-type ingenue toothpaste endorser and takes his place. Absently he runs his hand through his hair, clears his throat, waits patiently for the host to motion him to begin, clears his throat once again and tells the assembled multitude, "I'm here to sell you *Flush*."

More applause as the train lights go on and the cars sidle into the Borough Hall station. Utterly spent, he says not another word until they reach the last stop.

Chapter 3½

OUR THANKS to Jeremy Haberman for bringing to our attention and allowing us to include his previously unpublished essay written in response to Granville Feidler's classic work of Hoffstetter criticism.

AFTERTHOUGHTS ON GRANVILLE FEIDLER'S "HOFFSTETTER: THE MAN BEHIND THE MASQUE, A CRITICAL INTRODUCTION"

Granville Feidler, in his widely acclaimed work, "Hoffstetter: the Man Behind the Masque, A Critical Introduction," has attempted in the space of two-hundred-fifty-six pages to give the reader insight and understanding into the novel *Flush*. To a large extent he has admirably succeeded, but the gaps in his scholarship are just as evident as the pleasantries.

If we pose the question, "Has Feidler contributed to our enjoyment and/or understanding of the work?," the answer must be considered affirmative. His brief anecdotes are as readable as his style and enable the lay and/or serious reader to approach the novel with a heightened sense of who the man Hoffstetter really is. It is enlightening to discover that Hoffstetter rarely deleted, that some of his additions, with the inclusion of many vital sentences, were made while the manuscript was in printer's typescript; that the *seu*—Sue/Warren—*wiere* interior monologue may have been inspired by a letter he received from a certain author friend; that "before it was printed he tacitly deleted the Health Code chapter headings that appear in the manuscript." Much is speculation, but anecdotes are not evidences of serious interpretation; they are kernels of cocktail conversation, not signs of scholastic erudition. Of course, there is difficulty in understanding the first of these. Assuming that the statement "Hoffstetter is an artist" is a truth, it is easy to comprehend the difficulty of eliminating any written line or whole from a work-in-progress. From my own experience, I would surmise that Hoffstetter saw all of his work as a part of him, and it is not easy to cut away a section of what you have given your heart and love to, your *all* to, to add a clarifying point or rationalize a supposition with suitable additions.

Before turning to what may be termed "Feidler's Own and Sundry Epiphanies" re *Flush*, let us examine the scholastic lapses of this—our most fashionable—critic. Foremost is his failure to analyze the work in terms of the Aquinian denominator, a philosophic definition of that which comprises a work of art. According to Arden K. Hoffstetter, a thing of beauty is achieved through "an ecstatic stasis." This requires "Entity, eurythmy, and effulgence." Although Feidler shows that Hoffstetter has imposed "a static ideal upon motive material," he does not respond to the three values given by Aquinas, values which he ponders over, but upon which he fails to make any definite statement.

Entity is achieved through a unification of parts. Eurythmy is created when the organic whole works, that is to say, when the parts mesh so as to achieve a consistent end. Effulgence: well, the life force, according to theosophists, endowed all living creatures with an aura, a rosy light permeating through and surrounding the body. Leaving the mystics aside, Hoffstetter's characters *do* come alive for us. We see Telly in his role as Everyman (or Everywoman), come to understand and sympathize with him, for as Feidler contends, he manifests sentiments in us through which "the more we comprehend the causations which frustrate them, the more we empathize with his frustrated emotions and/or actions." On page 450 the organic wholeness of *Flush* is clarified, but the harmony and radiance are not.

Secondly, "'Art,' said Arden K., 'is the human and inhuman disposition of sensual or prurient matter for an ecstatic end.'" Aquinas, through Arden K.'s interpretation, denotes beauty in terms of those things which are pleasing to the sight and satisfy the appetite. Again, Feidler misses an opportunity to analyze Hoffstetter in terms of his own (as Arden K.) criteria for art and beauty. *Flush* is aesthetically pleasing, purely in terms of its fluid and unique word poetry. The final page is just one of the many examples of Hoffstetter's preoccupation with language, and the beautiful and often eerie results which he was able to achieve. "All of Hoffstetter's characters have something of his own preoccupation with the mystique of the written word." But much of this work is not pleasing to the sight. The ugliness, the paralysis, the grotesque, are all shown in graphic terms. The wide spectrum of sight never converges, but runs rampant from inquiries into the nature of decaying piscine cadavers to the sublime evocation of "how she tongued me under the *pissoir* wall." Does *Flush* satisfy the appetite? Feidler does not let us know. But, of course, it must be remembered that today Feidler is no longer considered the last word on Hoffstetter, and it takes a better definition of "appetite" to comprehend the point. We are fully satiated when we reach the final page, stuffed as it were with nearly three thousand pages of life, obscure pedantry, dazzling displays of stylistic hyperbole, and human pathos.

If these be flaws, they are just about concealed beneath what I have previously denoted as the Feidler Epiphany. Feidler has tried to enter into the realm of the artist's own consciousness in an attempt to unravel the various motivations which went into the writing of such a work as *Flush*. In this, his success is complete. There is great validity when he writes that, "*Flush* signalizes a shift and adjustment in viewpoint from the personal to the epic; it leads the writer away from himself and his own denigrating id toward an exploration of the libido of the bourgeoisie." To paraphrase Feidler, Hoffstetter has attempted to fuse the introspection of *My Secret Life* with the exteriorized landscape of *The Pearl*. "It masterfully attempts to subject the city-dweller to a process of sexual transfiguration."

His analysis in terms of the Health Code motif is always illuminating, giving the reader a rich background for understanding Hoffstetter's intentions. Particularly helpful is his explanation of the opening pages of the Sewage Disposal Plant episode. Each fugal note is given its meaning as, for example: "'Plip. Plop.' Telly, with a sigh of deceit, hears Ingersoll depart." Rereading this section I was able to follow the author's complications; understanding was achieved by using a simplistic key which Feidler provided. The novel was that much more valuable.

For the most part Feidler is fully in favor of what Hoffstetter has done. The exception is the *Croton Bug* chapter, where Feidler contends that the literary parodies are conscious Hoffstetterian pedantic conceits. That we cannot take seriously the idea that they "illustrate the principle of organic decay," reduces Hoffstetter's use of the imitative *(pastiche)* form "to a middling absurdity."

Hoffstetter's premise, says Feidler, that language and appropriate word spacing can imitate any given physical immediacy by exact duplication of a verbal sound or effect, "lures him into a confusing *ménage à trois*." Of course, knowing that this *mélange des genres* was premeditated, it is easy to justify Hoffstetter as the one author who most wanted to convey the very essence of sexuality. But, nevertheless, the *ur-Flusschen* sequence is connotatively as opaque as the *mélange* of Malory, Browne, Dickens, Joyce, Salinger, Carlyle, *et al.* employed at the Croton aqueduct.

Wonderfully succinct is the conclusion that the form of Hoffstetter's book is "a sincerely naive and eclectic Orgasm of its age." Mix liberally doses of the montage of the cinema, the impressionism of the French school, the Wagnerian leitmotiv, Jungian psychoanalytic free-associative techniques, Krafft-Ebing metaphors and Latinisms, and the philosophy of Masters and Johnson. "Take of these elements all that is malleable and perhaps more, and you have the style of *Flush*." As an ardent admirer of Arden K. Hoffstetter's work, I would like to think that there was something else, something besides the "perhaps more" that goes into the final making of this great work of contemporary literature. The Hoffstetterian mythos merges with the Health Code leitmotiv. From the two, the organic whole, the synthesis and recombination, the new and original, has arisen, and from it a work of power and depth, one which will certainly survive its century.

Chapter 4

"CHINGA! CHINGA!" shouted a swarthy, greased, and little man who ran alongside the station platform, enunciating in a most chéful way as Arden K. and Belinda stepped out into the sunshine. (Later, Arden would recall that the elevated platform was as close to the sky as he had gotten all day.)

"What's he saying?" Belinda asked her friend, noticing in the air a smell that was quite different from Yorkville and the East Side.

"Maybe he wants us to hire him. You know, tour guide and rickety scrimshaw to rent. That sort of thing." He stuck his hands deep into his trouser pockets where there was no change to jingle, carried his ontological argument one step further—ready to indulge the well-traveled and travailed-upon Thespian in computatious high jinks of jinrikishas and kickshaws, all the while moving adroitly as he followed the prominently arrowed instructions which led down to the street.

They were on Rutland Road, at the corner of Sutter Avenue, and from where he stood Arden could see the bright blue letters of the movie marquee glistening across the street. CERULEAN STUDIOS—Fabricators & Erectors since 1946. The name spelled out capitalism, the free enterprise system and an avid detachment from its shabby surroundings, and Hoffstetter remembered that Guysman's operations were now housed in the site of the old Sutter Theater.

(At this junction, not yet crucial, let the lay suburban reader be duly informed that Arden, not having spent his childhood musings along these boulevards, could not feel the slight wistful pangs that accompanied the waking hours of former patrons of this renowned cinematorium. Alas, the 25¢ Saturday matinee: double feature, Pathé newsreel, and five cartoons had gone the way of the zany antics of Zazu Pitts, Abbott and Costello, the Edsel and, more recently, the Corvair.)

"This is where Norman Podhoretz grew up," he told the girl, proud to be able to share in the American heritage.

"So who's he?"

Was there disdain in her tone? He couldn't tell, but he said, "Never mind," for Arden was fast learning to put up with his neighbor's obvious lapses in scholarship. "Come," directing her to a candy store where an old man with assorted gray hairs coming out of each ear jingle-jangled the pockets of a neutrally shaded apron upon which were stenciled the names of long-vanished daily newspapers. "We'll have some of the native drink." He walked to the counter with touches of touristic and aggressive swagger sticking out of bounds and told the proprietress, "Two egg creams," beaming with obvious and uninhibited delight.

"Chocolate or vanilla mister?" she questioned without emotion, also wearing an apron like her partner—husband or father?—outside the door, this one a gay collage of assorted fruit syrups, maraschino cherries, and chocolate sprinkles.

"Chocolate or vanilla lady?" he repeated to Belinda, but she was too busy sifting and winnowing bits of esoterica from the slick undressed pages of an erotic publication to pay him much attention.

"Lady," the woman called out from behind the abortive security of the formica counter upon which huddled together boxes of forlorn and hardly used two-cent cookies and dead chocolate-covered cherries. "If you're not going to buy, don't touch the merchandise. And that goes also for the magazines."

Arden rapped her on the shoulder, whispering, "If you're not in the buying mood don't offend the natives." He looked back at the owner and finally made up his mind. "One of each." He watched her squeeze chocolate and then vanilla syrup into two old-fashioned coke glasses (ones he recognized as commanding a high price on the antique market), slurp in some milk from a container and finally stir the mixture as she added seltzer. The last he knew was identical to club soda, just carbonated water coming out of a fountain tap. She stirred vigorously and thrust the bubbling drink in Arden's waiting hand. A thick creamy foam poured over the sides. Arden remembered his primary ethnic readings and dug out two pretzel rods from one of the dusty cannisters, dipping one into each glass. He put down some change and handed a glass to Belinda.

"What're you giving me?"

"An egg cream. Very nutritious. It's supposed to be endemic to Brooklyn and Miami Beach," and they clinked glasses, swallowed as carbonated chocolate and vanilla milk made mustaches on and above their upper lips. Of the latter, one had been freshly shaved and after-shaved. The other had been delicately tweezed in various corner regions of the orbicularis muscle. Indeed, the girl was rather provincial in that she harbored a secret belief that depilatory agents, when used in excess, caused progressive sterility and/or birth defects.

For the moment, as the egg cream (origin of appellation etymologically uncertain) made its way down his throat and into his stomach, Arden recalled all the literary greats who had fashioned reality from the streets and stoops of the Brownsville neighborhood. The region's roots and origins were stuck into a past nearly as old as Manhattan's Lower East Side, but Brooklyn had—

through no fault of its own or its immigrants—become a place that people laughed about. For an instant he felt threatened, knowing that names like Roth, Malamud, Friedman, and Singer were in predominance, enjoying current vogue and winning the hearts of the reading public. He wondered if America would be ready to accept the ravings—subdued or otherwise—of a gentile author, if it had enough compassion and fiscal stamina to withstand the onslaught of a new voice, a spiraling noveling vision without prior sociological commitments. He wondered if there was enough cultural leeway left to allow the marked intrusion of a newcomer *goy*. Without arriving at an answer, Arden filed the question away for further future study and introspection, and began sucking the salt off the pretzel stick, delighting in the rare blend of gastronomic *non sequiturs* and calling attention to the logic of being too studied, too contrived in tone and outlook.

"Do you like Jews?" Belinda asked him in a secret voice as once on the street they stood beneath the shifting shadows of the elevated train.

"Whose?" he quipped, quite intentionally.

"Hebrews. The Chosen People. Of course, the element's changing, decidedly Afro-hispanic, but from what I gather, this place used to be just about *all* Jewish. Must have been an intolerably pushy place to grow up in."

He replied, "You sound like a bigot, young lady."

"Not necessarily," she went on, glad to have recovered her tongue. "Just an uptight anti-Semitic Jew. Perfect role for a lady editor in publishing."

"Well," although he failed to catch her private allusions, "they don't bother me. I mean, it doesn't matter one way or the other." Thinking, If she starts to get defensive I'll smack her in the teeth. "Actually," he continued, "there was only one Jewish family in my home town, but no one ever suspected until the postmistress let it get out—rather unceremoniously, I may add—that the

man was subscribing to the *New Republic*. For a while it
was just touch and go. Eventually, if my memory is still
accurate, they moved away and relocated in Chicago. One
of the fashionable suburbs, Skokie or Highland Park.
Then there was the time I thought I was going to marry
one. A girl from the yore days of college. Supposedly,
Jewish girls make the best wives. But nothing ever came of
it."

"I bet her parents must have died," Belinda said,
dipping out aphorisms with facetious abandon.

"I'd rather not talk about it," for the memory was an
unpleasant one and Arden would rather have this side of
past paradises, *his* past, slide away in a graspless
dreamland haze.

The light changed and few feet from a man in blue,
busy collecting saliva samples to use in a citywide study of
marijuana usage, the two of them reached the gilt portals
of Cerulean Studios only to find their way blocked or
blockaded by an unshaven picketeering trio, striking
members of the I.L.G.W.U. Fortunately for Arden (and
his future career, as later events which will be undiscussed
shall prove), he had never had a father who had been
active in the trade-union movement. Thus, he had never
been warned of the unpatriotic inadvisability of crossing
picket and scab-strewn lines. The placards strung about
the bull necks of what he supposed were weary stitchers
and cutters were lettered neatly, with union funds, and
Hoffstetter read the copy silently to himself: "B. Guysman
Enterprises Unfair to Organized Clothing," "Nudity is an
anti-union practice," and "Outlaw clothing and only
outlaws will go naked."

"What do you intend to do, freelancer," Belinda
inquired, kneading his shoulder with what he assumed
was uncommon delight.

Arden brushed her hand away as if a troublesome fly
had settled there, stepped up to one of the garment
workers, asking, "Would you be terribly offended if we

passed through? We're only visitors. We never go without a union label." He was surprised at his own brashness, because a second before making his introductory comments he had been seized by the same brand-X of terror he felt would have gripped him had he been called upon in a supermarket to distinguish (without visual aids) between oleo and the higher-priced spread.

"Show us," one of the men said gruffly.

It became immediately obvious to Arden that such discourteous conduct could not have come from an actual union member, accustomed as they were to gentlemen's agreements, and that these spotty-looking three were probably just hired to keep the picket lines going, their cause being one which was more than likely already lost.

"He'll do nothing of the kind," Belinda replied for him, taking up the defensive.

"Keep out of this lady; Women's Lib ain't welcome in Brownsville," a second intemperate voice added and Arden, catching a whiff downstream, suddenly realized that the men had been enjoying something a lot stronger than an Orange Julius for most of the afternoon. Teetotalism aside, Hoffstetter was not a great believer in the philosophy that everything done in excess was bad for the system, but he would not have his masculinity and self-respect threatened by a group of blackguards and insolent thugs.

"Out of the way," he told them, trading gruff for gruff and steering Belinda's jersey-knit elbow past the signs and up to the gilt encrusted doors where once a kindly old gent who liked to goose little girls had stood taking tickets from the neighborhood youngsters and Golden Age citizenry.

The anti Anti-Saloon Leaguers were about to throw their combined weight around Arden K.'s body when the man in blue, on the lookout for new clientele, passed by and called out in a friendly fun-city way, "Everyone line up according to size places and spit." He waved a sample test tube above his head amidst the inebriated and insurgent growls of the men, linebackers temporarily foiled-again and put to triple shame.

Arden took the opportunity to open the heavy doors and once inside the two of them were stopped by a uniformed guard who demanded an immediate display of credentials and proper identification.

"We're the press," Hoffstetter explained.

"All the more reason," said the guard in his brightest remark of the day.

"Look, Mr. Guysman's expecting us," Arden said, tired of all the fun and games and anxious to get down to the work at hand.

"That's what they all say," the guard replied, starting to use his two meaty hands to repel their advance.

By now, Arden was in no mood to beat a hasty retreat. The dull hammer of fist against door was barely muffled by the acoustical tiles and rather than face possible and bloody harm, having no desire to contribute his paltry earnings to the plastic surgeon's art, he turned back to the guard and spoke his peace. "I demand to see Mr. Bernard Guysman. The matter is most urgent and should you prevent me in any way from completing my assignation, I shall have your uniform and studio privileges stripped off you as sure as my name is Arden K. Hoffstetter!" Granted, the language was a bit archaic, but Arden the intellectual snob felt that menials and subemployables had to be treated in much the same way as they were used to seeing portrayed on television and in the movies. Otherwise, they tended to get out of hand and would soon lose respect for their higher-ups.

The attendant sulked, thrusting out his badge-spangled chest like a pouter pigeon in great heat. Distress was evident; all these puffed-up incriminating charges would surely result in the revocation of his badge and his ultimate dismissal. So, albeit reluctantly, he led our two friends to his desk—occupying a position once enjoyed by the candy concession and hot buttered popcorn machine. He picked up the house phone and spoke sharply, feathers awry, into the receiver. "There's a pair down here wants to see Mr. G. Should I let 'em through?" He listened for a moment, curling his lips in a get-tough attitude and barked out to them, "What're your names?"

"Arden K. Hoffstetter and friend," still smarting from the inferior treatment he was getting and not enjoying.

"Arden K. Hatstealer and friend. Says he has an appointment. Okay, whatever you say." He hung up the studio phone and pointed to a grand marble staircase, curving out of sight beneath a thick cover of red-velvet carpet. "Up there and the girl at the reception desk will show you to B.G.'s office."

Poor Arden, prepared for both, had not received the injury concomitant to the insult. Perhaps he felt slighted, but we (whoever and whatever is none of your business) are unsure of this point and basic, pure and applied research into the matter have brought up little, if any, new and enlightening evidence. Therefore, let it be dispensed with and not trouble us any further, for—as is now well known—the lore of arcane details and suppositions is best left to ill-tempered lepidopterists and aging nympholepts.

An interruption in our narrative is considered advisable by our editor at this point—not necessarily to explain the meaning of our literary allusion which closed the last paragraph, mind you, but to brace you for the imminent introduction of a new character, a new *dramatis persona* previously mentioned by name only.

Screen Confessions magazine, now suspended from publishing by a court injunction and a show-cause order, has termed—and quite aptly—Bernie Guysman "the Guise Man." He is a man of many talents, chiefly that of reel and zipper manipulation, as well as an eye for the modishness of fads, or the faddishness of modes: either will do for now. Future generations of film devotees will best remember him for his shockingly original and revolutionary use of panning and subliminal flashbacks. Others will recall his favorite and highly stylized quasidocumentary 8mm and 16mm studies of tribadism in Paphian circles. It was Guysman who, denied any code or rating from the self-regulated motion-picture industry, brought his case to the Supreme Court and won an unprecedented victory with the landmark decision that anyone, regardless of sex, age, creed, or national origin, had the right to see smut if he or she so desired. What followed made American history. But that is years ahead of our story and, for the present and time being, the Guise Man contented himself with serving the needs of private art-film societies composed of sun worshippers, homophiles, heterophilic swappers, eunuchs, militant feminists, and assorted landed gentry. Of the latter, it need not be mentioned that the Princeton Rub Club predominated.

He was a kind man to those who knew him, a family man who, by renovating the old projection room, kept a spacious efficiency apartment for his aging mother right in the studio building. Often, visitors could be seen accompanying this controversial producing figure to Mrs. Guysman's retreat, to be served a rare meal of *matzo brei, kugel, pirogen,* or other such Eastern European delicacies. It was a studio joke of long standing that when Mrs. Guysman stuck her head out of the projectionist's booth and yelled, "Bernie! *Bernele!* Time to eat," all filming stopped and everyone took off an hour for lunch.

Such was the congenial atmosphere surrounding Cerulean Studios. Although disagreements frequently arose amongst B.G. and his employees, these were simply put down by a sharp cuff on the ear. Guysman could not abide insubordination and in return for a kind of filial loyalty, a patriarchal awe, he gave his workers various progressive and nonunion benefits: health and pension plans, three-week vacations, paid maternity and abortion leaves, and so forth. All these devices endeared him to many. His camera crews were fiercely devoted to this rising entrepreneur. His actors came and went, for as has been previously voiced by one of our supernumeraries, there was really no future in dirty blue movies.

The great man himself rose from his chair, placed one hand on the flat polished surface of his desk and extended the other in a benevolent wave of good cheer and camaraderie. "Mr. Hoffstetter, I presume," with the well-meaning sweet consistency of a charlotte russe.

"It is indeed a pleasure to finally get to meet you, Mr. Guysman," our Arden began, thankful that he had left Belinda outside in the waiting room to cross her legs coquettishly and scan the pages of past issues of *Erect, Kiss,* and the now defunct and glossy *Eros.* "I have been an admirer of your work since first coming to this fair city."

If the cordiality was strained, Guysman made no mention of it, merely motioning him into a nearby chair and taking no notice of Arden's slight and evasive disappointment. The latter was a direct result of a box of Havana cigars having failed to materialize, for Hoffstetter assumed that all men in a position of power were able to obtain contraband even in these awkward contretemps. Nothing was opened, proffered, and waved before what would have been a most grateful set of smiling eyes. Instead, B.G. leaned back luxuriously in his executive throne and began chewing a Tums with great and thoughtful meditation.

"My story, my goals and dreams, are an open book, Mr. Hoffstetter," he began, rummaging in the top drawer of his desk and coming out with a small gold nail file. "All too often the press relishes the opportunity to discredit and disfigure a man of my imposing stature and position." He began cleaning his nails, dropping the under-nail dirt and shavings directly into an ashtray of cobalt blue glass. Arden, in turn, licked the stub of his pencil, unconscious imitator of much that he had seen and heard.

"The very same bluenoses and horny bluestockings," B.G. went on in his matchless sky-colored way, "who love to rip my films to metaphorical shreds are, all too often, the very people who maintain a secret and well-stocked library of the most irreverent pornography imaginable. *Filth*, Mr. Hoffstetter! They thrive in private places on the very filth they find in all that is free and decent, liberated and honest. Uninhibited! The denial of sexual liberties by these vicious, sick, and frustrated libertines is, in my qualified estimation, one of the most serious and tragic hazards facing our society today. Don't you agree?"

"Most definitely," he mumbled, busy taking semi-shorthand notes of all that was being said. He put down his pencil, concentrated for an instant on the milk-white slivers of discarded cuticle and nail, nodded his head and contributed on his own accord the following: "Most assuredly. Personally, I feel that the major cause of neuroses and mental disturbances in our culture is a direct result of this attack upon our sexual and physical freedoms. Inhibition is not natural, Mr. Guysman. It is, unfortunately, a learned act. When we learn to take the 'dirt' out of dirty books and French skin flicks, we'll all begin to breathe with considerably more ease than we are able to at present."

"Quite so. Quite so," the producer beamed, easily succumbing to Arden's ingratiating charm and masterful flow of words. "I see we share a kindred spirit, my friend, and that is most welcome, most welcome, indeed. And let me make it clear to you, right off, that I welcome this opportunity to air the linen, shall we say, to voice my heartfelt opinions and feelings and discuss my art with genuine candor. For it *is* art, Mr. Hoffstetter. Yes. Only art, true art, is capable of transforming our everyday realities into allegories of persuasive sexual and orgiastic myth. That is what Cerulean Studios is attempting to do today. This is what our work stands for. We are pioneers! Our films will survive long after we have made our plans and peace with our Maker. You may quote me on this," he dictated, eyes blazing with what Arden later considered to be satyric glee.

A single newly cleaned and pared finger stabbed at the air, emphatic reminder of the power behind these words of agitation. "We stand for the moral resurrection of pride in the divine act of copulation. Not necessarily procreation, mind you. But the joy which is inherent in the physical and spiritual release of one's sexual being. My films, all of them in one way or another, depict a segment of this ever-emerging sexual landscape which surrounds us all. They share this common statement, this common meeting ground. To liberate, to release, to ultimately serve as a vital tool for public and parochial education."

Arden's writing finger caught up with the speech in time, just barely, to write down the next fervent burst of dialectic. He flipped to a clean sheet as the Guise Man continued.

"Perhaps you would like to view an actual filming? Right now we're working on an updated version, revival so to speak and as it were, of *Little Women*. Of course, Louisa May left much to be desired, but with a fresh approach and a new title, I think the public will greatly appreciate our saucy historical efforts."

"What is the name of this film, may I ask?" knowing that editors like facts, rather than generalizations.

"The working title, which I think we'll use for the final edited product, is *Girls Will Be Girls*. Subtle, don't you think?"

"An excellent choice," Arden replied, surprised at his own sense of amusement. "It would be most useful for my article if I would be able to see your studio in actual operation."

"Fine. Fine," said the Guise Man getting up from his desk and rearranging his paunch.

"One problem," trying to solicit a sympathetic

response to his shy reserve. "I brought along a friend of mine, a rather charming young lady who has her heart set on the stage. I hope you don't mind if she accompanies us."

"Not at all. It will be my pleasure."

Once outside the office, where the monochromatic azure hues had taken their toll on Arden's visual acuity, he went through the socially regimented routine of necessary introductions. Guysman eyed the girl for a few silent seconds, then advised, "I have room for you, Miss Blumright, in the inner working of this organization. We'll dye your hair, bill you as our latest find, our very newest and *au courant* underground star. How does the name of . . . let me suggest . . . Mercura Chrome sound to you? There's a great future in this business. Plenty of room for advancement ever since we did away with the old star system by putting the dressing rooms on a communal basis."

Belinda, appearing to be uncomfortable at being addressed and mentally undressed all at the same time, replied in a low and carefully controlled tone, "Thank you for having so much confidence in me, Mr. Guysman. But right now I'm channeling all of my creative energies toward the legitimate stage. Perhaps we can work out something at a later, and more indefinite date."

"You're making a big mistake," with sorrow more applied than felt. "But, there's no need to make any definite or concrete decision right at this moment. You have my number. Call at your convenience." Nevertheless, after walking ahead for a step or two, he turned back and gave Belinda another look, another overloaded and thorough going-over. "Did you say your name was Blumright?" he asked at last.

"That's right."

Guysman snapped his fingers. "Of course!" he said with delight. "I thought I recognized you. Didn't we meet at . . . ?"

"Nowhere!" Belinda hissed. "You must be mistaken. I've led a very sheltered life."

"But I'm sure...."

"Quite impossible." Arden thought he heard her mutter, "Idiot," under her breath, but he wasn't quite sure and stayed close to the producer, as if that was where the money was.

Avoiding the staircase from whence they had first arrived, most uncelebrated of entrances when remembered retrospectively, B.G. led the Yorkville commuters to a private elevator. The three of them squeezed inside the narrow car and Guysman pressed a button marked *G*. As they descended, the cubicle riding slickly down its well-oiled shaft, Arden could feel a hand groping along his trouser leg. He shot a look at Belinda, bewildered and mute resentment was what you could call it, but her face registered nothing that could be considered even vaguely communicable. The grope reduced itself to a stroke of brazen insinuation into private places and the paunchy figure explained:

"After we finish this one we're going right into production with what I think will be my most significant contribution to the art of film. A most impressive venture, Mr. Hoffstetter. It's called *Law and Order on the Indiana Thruway* and will be filmed entirely on location. Sound stages are far too confining for a production of this scope and magnitude. I intend to film a cohesive statement on the violence in our American way of life, dramatizing all the forces which work toward the downfall and destruction of highly littered specialized civilizations. There will be sidesplitting side steps into the problems of the generation gap for comic relief and, of course, the vastly untapped resources of the New Pornography. You'll get to meet the star, a really remarkable Stanislavskian whom we've imported directly from Japan. He's actually an Ainu, and his screen test was the most brilliantly conceived and hirsute adorned study of liberated raw masculinity I've ever had the pleasure to view. He's even consented to teach my mother the tea ceremony, that's how considerate he is. In fact, the fellow, quite a giant in his own right, is most suited for portraying hairy, hostile kinds of love. A veritable yeti, you'll see."

Arden was not overjoyed by the promise, but kept his tongue glued to his palate and his pencil busy scrawling across his notebook.

A final, not altogether unpleasant goose delivered to his jewel box (a subtle family jest) and the elevator halted noiselessly. The door slid open and Arden was temporarily blinded by the stark searing brightness of arc lamps and Klieg lights.

"Try it again, Amoradá, and this time don't hesitate to use what god in heaven gave you. That's what we're paying you good money for."

"Blood money from the sweat of our brow!" yelled a voice from on high, somewhere in the vicinity of the second balcony.

"My mother," Guysman whispered, arching his neck and shouting out, "It's okay, sweetface. Everything's under control. Your *Bernele* can handle it. Don't worry."

Then the director sat back in his canvas-slung chair of modest proportions and the girl, bereft of any vestige of that hotly disputed union label, walked back onto the set: a room of white and chocolate brown, bare geometric designer pieces which heightened the voluptuous curving construction of her body.

Guysman leaned over, saying softly, "This is only kid stuff. Just a teaser we're releasing to introduce the Ainu to the general public." At that moment a door on the set opened and it seemed as if everyone suddenly froze in their spots, all space being temporarily solidified. The air was breathless, sliceable and pulsing with unmitigated wonder and desire. The door opened, the camera whirred on and out stepped an oriental gentleman, shades of east meeting west and hail to thee Commodore Perry, his imposing muscular figure swathed in a green silk kimono.

Clever, very clever, and artful indeed, Hoffstetter thought as he watched the drama and the actors begin to go through their paces.

Using Joyce's favorite earth colors to enhance the earthy quality of his new find, Arden K. said to himself as this vehicle of unabashed diversion unfolded before his eyes—which were, to say the least and leave it at that, considerably intrigued. The man is certainly on the ball, that's for sure, his inner voice went on. Probably even one step ahead of himself.

The green sash—an *obi* to crossword puzzle fans—was slowly undone by long kabuki fingers and the robe slid to the floor, white also and dazzling with fresh polish.

Guysman renewed his whispering with, "My mother forgot to put down newspaper, but they're barefoot so I suppose it doesn't matter," sighing with nocturnal (normal for the vast majorities of the population) longing.

But Arden was too dumfounded to hear. He coughed, choked on his amazement and turned his eyes away, shamefully aware of his own physical inadequacies. The Ainu bore an uncanny resemblance in particular parts to the famed Superstudman of legendary and pre-revolutionary Havana.

"A wonder bear, is he not?" B.G. asked, licking his lips with such noticeable and conspicuous delight that Arden K. now realized in a flash of putting two-and-two together, the source from which the previous elevator titillations had arisen.

He followed Guysman away from the sounds of animal (ursine?) arousal and noted the deference which Bernie G. was paid, as actors and film crews alike nodded their heads with respectful acknowledgment, moving with slavish asides so that their path and progress forward were quite unhampered and unimpeded.

At the other end of the sound stage Belinda, hair flying à la Julie Christie in *Darling* and cheeks freshly flushed, caught up to them. "He gave me his autograph!"

"And you're blushing," Arden said with disapproval, detecting in her eyes the most nasty and naked of emotions.

"I'm getting an education, Arden darling," she said between clenched uppers and lowers, so that our writer wondered if she had been taught to speak with a pencil between her jaws. He had been told by someone in the know, or had read in a firsthand account, that such practices—frowned on by the American Dental Association—were still common in various sections of affluent New England set aside under the auspices of conscientious philanthropists (or philandering misogynists) for the education and cultural country-club indoctrination of young boys.

"You're giving me a headache!" he snapped back, fearful that she would damage his rapport with the producer.

Belinda, still in her own little world, proudly revealed, "He let me touch it."

"Touch what?" said Arden in sudden panic.

"His kimono. Pure silk, really marvelous."

"Just don't make trouble," he went on with relief. "Remember, you're a guest!"

B.G. stopped at a door adorned with a gold-painted caption: LAPUNAR, Executive Writers Only. With a gesture of affection he put his hand to the knob, turned his head back and told them, "You have caught me in one of my rare good moods, Mr. Hoffstetter. Not everyone who visits us get a chance to view the peephole. Just a word of explanation, please, and then we'll go inside." He cleared his throat with self-conscious vigor. "In order to keep our writers aware and up on the current state of man's sexual proclivities, it was decided, almost two years ago, to establish the Lapunar. Here, behind a two-way mirror, my script men can view life under conditions of restrained actuality, rather than having to resort to their own mental or creative imaginations. The latter, I may hasten to add, often tinged with personal...idiosyncrasies, shall we say. The peephole caters to no one taste. On the contrary, for it reveals a full spectrum of exchanges between upwards of three and four consenting adults. When I first dreamed of this little arena, this psychodrama...."

"This sexually secular scriptorium," Arden interrupted, tapping out a rhythm and always prepared to turn a catchy phrase as his pencil scribbled across the notebook page with a sudden burst of gusto.

"Precisely," B.G. agreed, continuing with a rising momentum. "The games or activities—no different I imagine—are ongoing from nine to five with, of course, an hour off for lunch. Initially, I thought of this room in terms of a laboratory of living. If you'll check your notes, Mr. Hoffstetter, you'll remember how I spoke of my desire to capture and subdue and thereby transform reality onto a higher and more permanent level. I would now go so far as to say that without the intrinsic benefits of the Lapunar, my writers would grow stale and stuffy in no time at all. I have no room in my organization for trained hacks, Mr. Hoffstetter. Through a careful use of the peephole and the forces contained therein, my films need never grow repetitious or smug. And,"—the 'furthermore' implied in his florid expression,—"the room serves the dual function of limbering up my new actors, getting them loose and returning them to a kind of methodism, an *au naturel* way of reacting to scripts which rely heavily on the power of dramatic improvisation. Indeed, many a star was born inside this little bedroom."

At that he turned the knob of the door and stepped within, beckoning them to follow and saying brightly, "As you'll see, the bravest *must* do more. It's only right."

Once, Arden K. had complained to a friend whose sympathetic mooncalf eyes encouraged him to be honest, that there was nothing to write about. He dreaded resorting to fashionable and cute little literary tricks, like filling in a transition scene by staging a dwarf's wedding.

The friend, who was by no means a congenital idiot despite the ingenuous quality of his eyes, had replied in his usual plaintive and woebegone manner—for he was an artist who suffered from color blindness—that it was quite unrealistic of Arden to look upon or think of himself as a writer when he had lived so little, and had seen far less.

At this, Arden K. struck a defensive posture, declaring, "Experience and sight-seeing do not, my dear friend, make a great writer. A man can live all his life in one little room, know only the people who inhabit his particular tenement, but if he is able to understand and feel for humanity, he may produce a dozen novels of distinction with only the inhabitants of the tenement as his subjects.

"No, going off to faraway places in search of equally exotic viewpoints would not make me a better writer. The more one lives, the more one learns about others. The inner machinations, I mean. It is perceptivity and not grandiose experiences that makes a writer great."

The painter had remained silent, his manner deliberative until, at what he guessed was an opportune moment, he shunted the burden of his misguided dreams onto our demihero's shoulders. "Then it is up to you, Arden K., to make the choice between art—being that which stands for quality and reason—and notoriety, which, by the very nature of its countenance, can only lead you down paths which border along the river to Hell."

When the artist had departed, his monochromatic bespattered smock whispering and rustling upon his body, Hoffstetter had sat for a long while without moving, his features tinged with the pallor of sadness. He pondered the painter's closing remarks, thought deeply of the dangers that followed one who lusted after fame and success, money and power. At last he rose from his chair, drew himself fully erect and declared to the cat, who even then had refused to pay him much mind:

"I shall have both, cat. When fame arrives I will not allow it to dampen the quality of my prose. The two shall go hand in hand, one forged onto the other. If Lord Byron, Picasso, and Leonard Bernstein can do it, well...so can I!"

Provincial resilience: the initial shock would wear off within minutes—had not he first paved the way for techniques of avant-garde drama back in those distant Branch and budding days?—but it would be months and many moons before Arden K., visitor and unwitting voyeur, would be able to discuss the affair of the Lapunar with any degree of verisimilitude. And then it would not occur during a direct interpersonal confrontation, but rather via his typewriter as he sat at his desk and worked on the long-neglected article drawn from notes and quotes taken at Cerulean Studios.

Surprisingly, the essay was largely ignored by the discerning public and no legal proceedings were ever brought up against our client.

At the moment the door was opened, it appeard that the participants in the producer's *tableau vivant* were rapidly approaching a fourway simultaneous release, a rare departure from societal norms in (excuse the pun) more ways than one. Properly, they were heading down the orgasmal road, with a dripping red-hot sunset not in the far-distant future. Liberated as he may have thought he was, Arden broke into an involuntary cold sweat, conscious of the fact that there was nothing he could do to contain his enjoyment and pleasure in viewing the complicated acts unfolding before him. He buttoned his jacket and folded his hands, concealing his embarrassment.

Guysman was grinning, his meaty hands dug into the maw of his pockets, secretly kneading the root of his mixed-type psychoneuroses. Of this and these, Hoffstetter was unaware, despite his writer's eyes. But he felt dirty, used, cheated out of any form of decency or propriety. He avoided glancing at Belinda his quest-mate, knowing that she too was more than likely enraptured and momentarily hypnotized, spellbound by what millions of horny Americans dared admit only in the privacy of their dreams.

It is not our intention to use this event as a rationalization for going into a blow by blow description of such Frequent Use of Carnal Knowledge. Readers who need their memories refreshed are urged to take this opportunity to consult Sellon's classic study, *Annotations on the Secret Writings of the Hindus* (London: Printed for Private Circulation, 1865).

Suddenly, as the animal sounds reached a Stravinsky-an crescendo, discordant as chalk on a blackboard, Belinda collapsed to the floor, twitching slightly and with good reason. Arden K. cupped his hands over his ears, blotting out the blasting and noisy pleasures of multiplied hedonism. His eyes remained stuck: a doll broken in the act of saying a four-letter colloquialism not mentioned by persons of quality. The lids refused to cower, to close and turn away with shame, so that Hoffstetter saw all and later, would remember far more—right down to the last drop. But he couldn't decide if it was good or not, although it almost tasted, smelled, and looked like the real thing.

Chapter 4½

ADDITIONAL background material for the official unauthorized biography of Arden K. Hoffstetter.

One threatening mud-colored evening, during a three-day weekend when her husband had gone out to the Coast on pressing business, we strode into the gaily lit and opulently decorated lobby of Chicago's once most famous highrise, Marina Towers, those twin cylindrical apartment buildings from whose heights many a suicide has stood, swaying slightly and transfixed, awed by the magnificent view of Lake Michigan and the Loop. Here in the city now immortalized by Saul Bellow, James Purdy, *Medium Cool*, and Lynne Kaufman—my brother's old girlfriend—we had come all those miles to visit and chat with Eileen Priscilla Dubrow, Arden K. Hoffstetter's one-time college steady and sometime sweetheart.

Mrs. Dubrow, known affectionately to her friends and intimates as "Trish," is a vigorous clubwoman, an active theatergoer, and the conscientious and doting mother of twin boys, lads by the names of Barry and Larry. Mr. Dubrow is a rising young certified public accountant with the firm of Klinger, Lewis & Baum and, according to his wife, "doing quite nicely and on the way up."

Our interview was just another example of the careful and exacting research we were putting into our account of Hoffstetter's life. Rather than having to resort to the use of secondary source materials, we had decided from the very first to approach our subject through those who knew him best. Of course, considerable clues into the author's fascinating and often shocking life can be obtained by a thorough exhumation of his *oeuvres*, but experience has shown us that people, rather than words, reveal truth far more readily and usually far more accurately as well. Hopefully, Mrs. Dubrow would not be the exception to the rule.

"I'll be out in a sec," said the bouffant hairdo in the Hawaiian wrapper, hurrying around a bend in the foyer and then out of sight. We took this opportunity to arrange ourselves and our writing tools in the living room, admiring the framed reproductions of Chagall, Keene, and Michelangelo which adorned the walls. The Dubrow living room, Country French and quite tasteful with imaginative touches of antique gold, marble, vinyl, and wax flowers, was the scene of our initial conversation.

"Of course, I'm really quite thrilled for him. You know, his success and all that," Mrs. Dubrow, in reply to our first question, remarked cheerfully, coming out of her boudoir in a raw silk suit, her eyes aglow with cosmetic magic. "I mean, of course I didn't think he was going to be famous...I mean, *this* famous, when we were sort of keeping company back then. But you never know, do you?" She giggled, covering a set of formidable buckteeth with the palm of her hand. "You know, I was young and innocent then. College was such a game. And even if I *had* known what the future would bring, which I didn't, needless to say, it never would have worked."

Pourquoi?

"Huh?" from the back of her throat and somewhat taken by surprise.

How so?

"Oh!" bilingualism not being her forte. "Things are a lot different these days than they were ten years ago," settling at the edge of a chair which faced the couch with the red and gold Chinese print fabric. "I mean, nowadays intermarriages are pretty common...among some

114

people. But then it just wasn't done. I mean, even in my own clique no one would have even considered it. My parents would have died if they knew that their grandchildren weren't going to be *bar mitzvah*ed. What else do they have in their golden years but the pleasure of going to affairs. My husband, Maury and I, are Reform, but my parents and his too—my *machetunim*—still keep the old ways."

Mrs. Dubrow passed around a box of chocolates, festive miniatures in gold-foil wrappers, returned to the lime-green crushed-velvet over-stuffed chair, saying, "We were babies. It was just innocent sorority stuff. I really wasn't ever serious. God! I hope Arden didn't tell you that!"

We assured her that we had not consulted Hoffstetter on the matter.

"Good, because sure I *liked* Arden a whole lot as a person. He was deep, you know. I always remember him being very deep and serious, almost moody, like he saw everything all at once and understood whatever happened around him. But he was never marriage material. He just wasn't substantial, like he dreamed too much. Understand?"

Did Arden K. ever discuss with you his own feelings or view about love, or what constituted love in his own mind?

Mrs. Dubrow bit into a chocolate, examined the bleeding center with a critical eye. "Frankly, I don't think he was really capable of loving, of going out into the world and earning a good living for another person. Maury always had his head on his shoulders. Even when he was a kid he worked part-time in his father's hardware store. He knew the value of a dollar from an early age. He sleeps in pajamas. He's that kind of person. I just don't trust people who sleep naked. It's kind of dirty, don't you think?" She was, of course, referring to the much quoted comment Hoffstetter had made to the reporter from *Life* magazine.

"What did we know from love? We were fresh college kids, not like the kids of today who'll do the real thing without even knowing what their last names are. Frankly, I'm sure that's the cause of all this violence and looting and that's why we have so many people on drugs and welfare. Arden, to be quite honest, just wasn't ambitious enough for me. Security's a very important thing in a marriage. . . ."

We could see that we were getting nowhere, memory having the property of dimming with the passage of years and babies, when the doorbell rang. Mrs. Dubrow jumped up, cursed the doorman for not having called up on the intercom, stabbed out her cigarette and hurried across the broadloom to the door.

"It's only the sitter," she called back, as if we were expecting to come face to face with the celebrated and hard working father of two. "Tonight's my mah-jongg night with the sisterhood at the temple," opening the door and admitting a typical North Shore high-school student. We put our notes away, slipped into our coats and hoped that Mrs. Dubrow would have a lucky and rewarding evening. She thanked us profusely, made us take a quick look at some recent candid 3x5 photographs of her two boys, and insisted that we take along the box of chocolates as they weren't good for her kids' teeth, anyway.

Cooperative as Mrs. Trish Dubrow had tried to be, she had unfortunately been unable to provide us with the necessary clues we were searching for. The Hoffstetter college years would thus have remained shrouded in mystery had we not been graced with a sudden and unexpected good fortune, an unforeseen kindness so typical of Chicagoans—thus earning them the admiration of people all over the world. Trish had gotten up in the middle of 3 dot and flower to call us at our room at the Wabash Y.M.C.A.

"Do you plan to see Arden's old roommate? she asked us, chewing on some unseen confection at the other end. Frankly, we were taken aback, having totally neglected to consider this aspect of our work. But Mrs. Dubrow came through, saving us hours of tedious legwork by volunteering the gentleman's name and what she thought was his last-known address. "Send him my best. Tell him Trishie Selig still carries a torch." Then the fire was extinguished and hours later, after a quick check in the telephone directory, we were driving in a gentle northeasterly direction toward the city of Detroit. More specifically, Grosse Pointe Farms.

Falderal Manor has been in the De Kidwell family ever since Marcus De Kidwell first settled there during the turbulent and closing years of the last century. Once a year the estate (which is famous for its definitive collection of early nineteenth-century Cornish chamber pots) is opened to the general public. The event is well publicized and always well attended, culminating in a gala masked charity ball that keeps Detroit society abuzz long after the last of the Chinese lanterns are taken down and put back in storage.

Lance De Kidwell came off the tennis courts wiping his face with a towel, a man of Hoffstetter's age with a ruddy complexion and a granite-lined face. He jogged across the spacious expanse of manicured lawn to where we sat overlooking the pool. Inviting us to join him for a Scotch, he began with robust good intention right off the top of his sandy and thinning Princetonian cut, "You might say that Arden Hoffstetter had heart. Here I was, a raw kid, fresh as the dickens, kicked out of Yale with nothing to my name but my family connections. Here was Arden, straight off the farm or just about. The two of us confronted each other and, most amazing of all, became fast friends. He's honest. I've always maintained that he was the one honest fellow I met when I was an undergraduate. Used to write my papers for me. A trifle quirksome, no doubt, but genuine. Giving. The genuine article, always around to help out a friend. No one could be more pleased for his success than I am."

Did he ever express any desire to be a writer when you knew him in college?

"The usual 'save the world' business. Nothing very serious," De Kidwell chuckled slyly. "Said he wanted to make a dent on people's consciences. He dabbled with a little poetry. You know, sensitive young man sowing his oats and pouring out his heart. To the best of my knowledge nothing ever came of it. Just the usual business. Sticky sentimental stuff. To be quite honest, I'm most surprised about all this sudden notoriety."

Meaning?

"Didn't think he ever had the drive," he told us, scratching the underside of his chin and hitching up his tennis socks. "Liked to dream. Can't ever forget the times I'd find him lying on his bed, just like that, lost in thought. Never thought he was a man of action. Not the go-getter type. Plodding, if you know what I mean. I liked Arden— don't get me wrong. I even respected some of the things he said, crazy as they were, but he never struck me as a fellow with spunk or any sort of dynamism. Not the kind who'd ever make it in private industry. But one thing, he *was* sincere, very real, very genuine. Not like half the others I used to rub elbows with."

Did he ever talk to you of his feelings about love?

Mr. De Kidwell reached for the bottle with a subtle tremble of his hand, turned his face away from us as he poured himself another libation, and said out of the corner of his mouth, "If you ask me, he loved Trish Selig. Never could stop talking about her. I remember he said that if she ever stopped seeing him he'd want to stop living. We've all heard that kind of business before. But with Arden it almost came true. Came the time Trish found herself a pretty decent-looking sheeny and she just gave Arden the ole heave ho, the old shafteroo. He wrote more poetry that semester than ever before."

And then what?

"What do you think?," as a slim girl with innocent colored hair and shrimp earrings came off the courts twirling sunflower-yellow crepe de Chine as only Detroit women can. "He survived," De Kidwell concluded, glancing once again at the unearthly beauty who moved silently across the grass. "He went on living. He graduated and you fellers should know the rest. Nothing ever comes from mooning around like a pup with your tail between your legs. Got to get it up and fight for what you want and what you believe in. I always told him that. 'Hoffstetter, get off your goddamn rump and show the world a thing or two.'"

At which point we rose from our deck chairs as De Kidwell introduced his wife. "Honey," he began again, holding her close to his sweaty body. "You remember Arden K. Hoffstetter, don't you? When I was at State. Remember? My crazy ole roomie. . . ." his eyes clouding over for a fraction of a second. "My ole roomie. My ole moonie roonie. . . ."

"Lance darling," putting down his glass. "I think you've had a very rough day at the club. I'm sure these gentlemen can see how exhausted you are. Wouldn't you like to go into the house and take a nap before dinner?"

Before we could make our good-byes, De Kidwell suddenly broke into a smile. "Guess he did. Guess he showed 'em all, even me. Even doubting ole me. Guess he really made it this time."

We thanked him warmly and found our car where the butler had parked it alongside the servants' quarters. Drawing no allusions, it was decided that we would spend the night in Detroit visiting with old friends before heading back East the following morning.

Chapter 5

THE SKY had turned a piercing bloodshot blue—supreme inversion—when Arden and Belinda took leave of Guysman Productions and passed once again through the doors of Cerulean Studios. Arden K. squinted even though the sun was lowering, even though the studio had been well and brightly lit. He did this out of habit, recalling and reclaiming in a back-in-time flash the days he had sat in the balcony of the Bijou Theater, wads of chewing gum stuck under every seat. Saturday matinees with his lunch in a paper bag (a "sack" as they called it in Hometown), double features and coming out with his eyes smarting from the glare to streets that were emptying as stores pulled down their blackout shades and locked up their wares in defiance of the sanctified security of church Sunday. Like so many boys during those early post-war years, he had tried to pattern his life over a cinematic terrain, preferring the stark trick-shot landscapes of Orson Welles rather than the expansive musical journeys of Bob Hope and Dorothy Lamour. But such habits pleased him, as if he could contain within his heart lost moments of his boyhood, moments which—in some preternatural way—formed a link between what he had once imagined and what had finally come to pass.

They walked in the direction of the subway station, retracing their steps, collecting their movements unknowingly so that if anyone should try to follow them they would have to work by scent alone. They said nothing to each other, either too embarrassed or too absorbed in their own accumulation of past images to wish to communicate. Alone inside himself, Arden resurrected the last scene Guysman had allowed him to witness. *Girls Will Be Girls*, that childhood dimpled mainstay made over now into something he had yet to decide was either cynically vulgar or else unparalleled for its insistence that decadence was the final cesspool toward which all of our civilization and technocracy was flowing, to end up in a sump of moral, spiritual, and emotional decay. For he saw now, even as the street crowds jostled around him doing their dance of sexual avoidance, that uncharted choreography of side-stepping zigzags, that he had become—in some small but significant way—part of all the grotesque distortions and macabre depictions to which Guysman had committed his art.

The set was simple, perhaps even deceptive. A modern *House & Garden* kitchen with standard appliances. A white wall phone and a high kitchen stool, wall cabinets within a finger's reach. The phone rang. It was Mrs. March. The girl lifting up the receiver was Jo. Mrs. March told her that Beth had died.

How?

Lupus.

Oh, one hand disengaging itself from its former and as yet unseen task to open the Hollywood cabinet door, examine a bolt of black cloth, close the door again, and continue listening as the camera angle changed, continued to move an electric vibrator—unmistakable symbolism—in and out, in and out...

Guysman had told him that at this point words would be flashed on, superimposed upon the screen. "Exciting stimulation with the Cordless Personal Massager-Vibrator. Use anywhere on the male or female body. 7 inches long, 1½ inches in diameter. ONLY $2.95. Batteries (2) 40¢. N.Y. residents add tax. Send check or M.O. to..."

"What do you think?" thumping him on the shoulder as if that was where such processes took place. "A real pisser, right?"

"Groovy." So sublime. So cautioned. So lacking in feeling. And what had Belinda said about selling out? And the thought: Is it possible to die in the midst of all that pleasure by sudden freak electrocution?

His stomach was strong. Not as young as it used to be, but still in fairly good and unulcerated working order. He wondered if the statement was accurate, surrealistic to the point of searing and horrifying truth. Or wisdom. Death and masturbation, self-abuse and self-gratification, even as another grows cold. What shall I wear tonight? muses the naked child, breasts already budded into ripe handfuls of plastic pleasure. And he saw old men in forbidden movie houses covering their shame and identity with brown paper bags.

I must remember this, Arden K. thought. There is a clue here.

But of what and to wit he still had no idea, not even a notion of the frailest consistency, the lowest denominator.

His thoughts swung around once he found a seat on the train. Belinda hooked her arm through the crook of his elbow, nestled her head on his shoulder and seemed to fall instantly and thankfully asleep. But at such odd and sunny, such oddly sudden moments, on Sundays and on subways, Arden K. was prone to think of love, his love-life, and his life in terms of love. Such pangs of self-examination, self-incrimination, often afflict single writers and writer types of age thirty and above, coming and going with ever increasing and frequent regularity. Indeed, Arden K. was no exception to this grossly generalized scheme of things, this statement of our time and place. Perplexed by conflicting visions of cruelty and desire, strength and weakness, he tried to draw an order to things that hid within him, sequestered things unsaid and sometimes forgotten. His longings, in retrospect, seemed innocent, naive as a child's, some immature facet of his nature that dared to experiment with allusions of reality, dared to write about a mother who didn't love her child. A child's plaything universe, with furniture and adults rearing up with faulty and inaccurate proportions, and always the promise of some utopian paradise hanging over the vista of the future, compelling him to grow up, move on, step forward.

He began to dream of femme fatalities. There had been only one.

State. The U. The Campus. The quad.

Three point two beer night after night. A heavy date. Booking.

A girl with buckteeth who listened.

No longer did he have to talk to walls, to trees, to clouds, or solely to himself, an ego dependent on feedback. For he loved this creature who sat before him, buttering his muffins, eyes ablaze, absorbed in listening. This creature who nodded her head, communicated her interest by subtle movements, her face and body wavering, twisting in deference to his words. The syntax is all. Trish Selig. Shaker Heights. Money. Spoiled child of post-war plenty . . . ah, symbols dripping, slipping in and out as dream visions inundated his subconscious. Love is the denial of self. Losing an ego in the process. The "I" dissolving and merging into something new. And what happens if it only works one way, if in the end you are left with a pool of liquid ego as the other goes merrily on her way?

Maury's coming up for the weekend. I just want you to know.

Maury who? What Maury?

Oh Arden, I told you . You remember. The accounting major.

I don't want to remember.

Thinking, thoughts within thoughts: How did I ever

get involved with a girl who lacked compassion? All she's good for is nodding her head and hiding her deformed dentures with the palm of her hand. You'd think with all their money they'd have invested in orthodontia.

I don't know why you look so surprised.

I never expected to be treated so shabbily, like a nothing.

But Arden, you have your dreams. Your dreams will keep you company, even when everyone else is gone.

Had she ever said that? he wondered now. Or were things left unsaid, undone, two people slipping away from each other, reaching a moment in time when they relayed their awareness of each other's existence by a nod of the head, a half-baked smile.

Show the world a thing or two, Arden ole man. Give 'em hell.

Lance. Ferdelance. Lance de Ceitful.

Writing papers for him for Business Ethics, Mass Communications. What did I know from money-making, just favors for a friend. Unjust favors for a back-thumper, a handshaker, a label-reader. I have no use for people who use each other, borrowing quotes and thoughts with no intention of returning them, stripping someone of their very identity and making them look like the fool in the eyes of others.

And the dream cosmos exploded, silver castles in the sky as only a maker of rhymes, a twister of verses can see them, d-lysergic acid diethylamide tartrate self-manufactured so that his hallucinations, like the saints and apostles, came from within, from nature's own pantheistic light. Reserved for kings and gods, fools and poets. The godhead now unfolding through the crystal haze of lines of force, geometric special vibrations good and bad, comes a dais in a shimmering banquet hall where wine poured like mead and oaken tables were covered with cloths of fine-spun linen.

And now, it gives me great pleasure to present this

year's winner of the coveted National Book Award for fiction, a dear friend and a great craftsman, the author of the masterpiece that has so overwhelmed us all, Flush, *Arden K. Hoffstetter.*

The last drowned out in wave after wave of deafening applause as he mounts the platform, accepting with a grin the handshakes and smiles, eyes lowered with soulful humility, modesty personified.

The sleeping Arden smiled. The dozing Arden breathed deeply and heard himself making a speech of grateful acceptance, words forever anthologized but lost now as a locker-room smell of packed bodies filled the subway car, the crush reaching deadly proportions.

Death defying...and it began with an awakening scream.

"We exist on a sexual landscape of such ornate phallicity as to make the act of chewing on a pencil stub appear, on the most elementary level, obviously castrative," says Telly, Arden K.'s alter-hero demiego, in a burst of rare insight sometime during the course of events encompassed in the paged universe which is *Flush.*

For the purpose of this rigid analysis, it is now known that the idea of the sexual landscape—so important to any complete study of Hoffstetter's novel—came to him one rainy afternoon. Having purchased a bunch of fresh young California carrots as well as other choice items for his table, our young friend boarded the Third Avenue bus considerably dampened, if not in spirit then at least in appearance. He sat across from a woman who wore her plain gold wedding band on the right finger of her wrong hand, as well as an imitation lizard-skin plastic raincoat, in a shade of iridescent aquamarine. Her long narrow umbrella was blue, with a matching slipcase.

The shopper, caught in the storm or caught in a state of dishabille, seemed overly anxious to cover her umbrella and she twirled the collapsed struts together, slipping the snug fitting cover over the wet polished tip of this protector against the elements. Her hands looked ravaged, as did her face, either with too much work or too much love-making. Arden could not be sure. She edged the slipcase down the umbrella shaft and Hoffstetter, his attention drawn to the movements of her hands and fingers, watched with decided interest. For as the woman pulled the case down along the length of her *parapluie*, her hands moved swiftly, her wrists making gentle caressing arcs with a clockwise motion. Arden noted the care with which the task consumed her. No wrinkles were tolerated; the material was pulled taut and clinging, perfect from every angle. And the wrist kept circling, something familiar in her gestures, the bumbershoot (as they say in affected circles) resting securely in the palm of her hand. He could not take his eyes away, nor fail to draw the most basic, the most obvious of analogies after being witness to this performance for the length of time it took the bus to go from East 57th Street to the corner of East 73rd.

I give a mean hand job, her actions seemed to say with gusto, considerable pride as well. I don't miss a trick, not a stitch. Did you ever see such fluidity of motion, such care and exquisite grace. My calluses are all in the right places. For, as my hubby used to say, it's almost as good as the real thing, almost too good to be true.

When the woman looked up, the nylon satinized cover buttoned into completion, Arden K. stiffened, felt her eyes bore into his soul and retreated. He turned his face away to peer out of the rain-spattered, dew-splattered window, hungry for candid glimpses of urban life out there in the glistening damp.

An awakening scream: for starters.

Nothing. No amount of reading or living, even if one could be an excuse for the other. Nothing, would or could have prepared him for this. What is to follow. And should not be construed as a fictional necessity, but rather as an inevitability born of a desire to ... please no one, not a one in particular.

Hard to get one's breath, even now with all that madness, screaming, pushing stampede of blood and noise.

Panic. I arrive. I am here. I burst quick as a wink through the conventional bonds of this narrative, paper, ink, and glue, this our storytelling vision: a voice without a name, to stare at you with fright (crying? nothing is ever right). To mirror Arden K. in these minutes of dilemma, for we do love him mightily, so mightily. To re-reflect his mounting anxieties in the face of growing outside agitation. Proper intellectual bigots and snobs—we. For I am reminded of rats in a cage. A wire cage whose dimensions, *sans* water bottles and shredded newsprint litter, never alter, never change. Going berserk when conditions become too crowded. Murine muridophagy! Rat cannibals! Simple as that. And, too, the wounded cries of feral children, heard in dark forest places by the chosen and promised few. Feral babies nursed by vixens and she-wolves, who cannot be trained—not even to wash toilets and the insides of public lavatories—once they have reached puberty. You must get them out of the forest if you want them to grow up socially useful, get them out of the meadows and glades before the follicles ripen, before the blood begins to flow and Mommy is not there to explain the hidden mysteries of life. These sylvan lost ones shall be the subject of my next novel. A novel novel in and out of contemplation. An amusing curio, we daresay.

I mean to confuse because the following events have hardened, angered, amucked my soul.

They said: it took two hours for the media to get wind of the story.

They said: it took four days to identify all the victims. Four days before all of the loved ones came forth to claim their own.

They said: it took two weeks with welfare mothers

working double shifts to remove the last and first traces of blood and day soil from the car. From the seats, the walls, the windows, the floor of this underground vehicle of death and gore.

I will be silent shortly and say no more. I should never have spoken out of turn, out of context. It is not proper, nor fitting, nor considered good form and the form is all. So I shall return you to Arden who sees things much as you would (had you been there); for he is so much like you, is he not?

And, before closing. This is not a mystery story. Do not feel obliged to refrain from discussing this chapter until your friends, acquaintances and procreative partners have read as many pages as you have. Do not feel obliged to chastise us because we have broken the ring of chilling suspense, if such a chill or such a ring were ever there. To tell you the truth: a thriller was the last thing we had in mind.

We return then to that scream, a jarring high-pitched string of notes echoing over the third rail, bursting Arden K.'s fatuous dream bubbles as Belinda too jerked upright, her nails raking across the inside of his arm where the skin was most tender to the touch. The straphangers pressed down on him, their faces hidden, the minds and sense organs of the labor pool turned collectively toward the source of sudden terror. Indeed, the shivering and goose flesh accumulated bit by bit as now Hoffstetter caught sight of a man who had jumped onto one of the seats.

He had jumped onto one of the seats and had thrown down two women in their prime, bundles, bodies, and all.

See: glint of gun-metal gray over the horizon of ads for dandruff shampoo, toothpaste, and a deodorant for a woman's most private parts.

"Pull the emergency cord! Pull the cord!" as if they wanted to begin a new life with the same familiar screaming refrain. It was someone shouting very loud and Arden, not as frightened as he felt he should have been, knowing that for the time being Belinda and he were shielded by other bodies, thought of Dallas, Austin, and a beauty parlor in Mesa, Arizona.

(One learns to accept and expect madness in the Southwest as easily as hurricanes in Miami and a stock market slump originating in New York.)

The man on the seat yelled, "How are you fixed for life!" his voice rising above the din before it cracked and fell back on the ears of the breathers. And then the gun exploded. The trigger happy happy was pulled pulled pulled not with a jerk but with a squeeze, always on target that way, if your eye is good, and he smiled in orgasm, almost but not quite, wetting his pants as a damp stain blossomed on the front of his trousers. Another stain shone magically on the white shirt front of a somber gentleman wearing tweeds and *The Wall Street Journal.* Slowly the two stains, red and yellow, maroon and ochre, traveled outwards, almost merging, almost but not quite, as the man wilted.

Stem cut.

And fell.

Down down down to ground zero where there is no return. Shoe leather, dog spoor scented air. Ordure of the city wilds.

"Law and order! Give me law and order! Give it to us, baby! Sock it to us!"

But no one laughed. Not now. Not this time.

Arden thought that his turn would be next. With no room to hide, no place to crouch, he was startled by the sudden vision of his life: multileveled and multiterraced, flashing before his tear-filled eyes. The 2,500 pages of his novel, still without their ending, swarmed about him, his own words and phrases, his favorite literary conceits and metaphors, these and countless remembered images all taking flight. A surge of wingèd prosèd life, hurtling itself down upon him. A meteorite shower of disconnected words. A barricade, almost. Or a barrage. The meaning of his life was there as well, a protean shape glistening without definition, only inchoate purpose. He understood. And with this new-found awareness he gripped Belinda his dearest nearest friend, holding her tight, knowing that two hearts were far better than one as the gun ejaculated smoke and a bullet whistled through the hair, homing into the flesh, the mark, of yet another.

The Naked City dying one by one.

Ditties of Diddy, Front and Rear. "Diddy the Good . . . perceived the inventory of the world" as so much rubbish.

Another one of the nine million, each in their own way capable of rape and slaughter.

"Get the police! The cops!"

"They're all in cars. Not on the beat. Not on the street, and I am the freest of the free spirits!" said the madman with the metal organ. Two down and he searched for yet a third to make an unsmiling trio.

Arden looked through the press of bodies, saw the figure smile, saw the freckled thin skin of a red-haired man. With gun waving before him, his whole body elongated out of proportion like an El Greco saint, the man licked away a bead of sweat with the tip of his tongue, as another coursed down the hollow of one cheek.

Why wasn't anyone trying to prevent this? Why didn't someone try to pull him down? Arden wondered, thinking that perhaps in the narrow space between the subway cars there were many huddled half-escaped bodies, squeezed there to remind the authorities (later) of scenes similarly seen during fires at emergency exits which failed to open. Also between the cars: legs and arms flailing and thrashing wildly, limbs and torsos dragging along the tracks, crunching beneath the wheels which gave out tiny sparks of friction and electricity.

The noise.

Another scream and flesh sinking forward, the third one downed, falling onto his lap and he realized how close

he had been to death, how close he had come to the border
of his soul. His hands felt sticky, a warm dripping on his
skin. Too shocked to cry, his eyes suddenly dry. A desert
of tears with no release, no relief, no oasis in sight.

The cars lurched into the station, slowed down.
Pushing the crumpled body to one side he stands up on
legs that find it difficult to support his weight. Does the
conductor know? Is he aware as the doors open at 59th
Street and the panic swarms out, forward and away as the
last shot mingles with the faces of the still and many, the
open shocked eyes and mouths of disbelieving commuters.

A direct hit, this one. As were the others. Into the
russet auburn tipped face. Into his own mouth. And
Arden has seen it, has seen this final curtain-closer and he
blinks his eyes, afraid.

He would never write:

Dear Mother,

I'm sorry that I haven't written sooner but things,
as usual, have been rather hectic and I find myself
constantly pressed for time, always worrying about
how I'm spending it and where each minute is going.
But I did want to let you know that I am alive and
well, especially in light of events which took place
yesterday.

Yesterday on the subway a man went berserk.
(There, I've *said* it and maybe now I'll breathe a
little easier.) Really insane like a lunatic or a
maniac. He went out of control and before anyone
could stop him he had ended his own life and had
caused the demise of three others, all total strangers.
The whole sorry spectacle took place on the IRT
train as I was coming back from Brooklyn. Mother, I
have never been so frightened, so out of my senses

and utterly, absolutely speechless. Never in all my life, and you know very well that I am not particularly prone to bouts of exaggeration. I was reminded of Father's funeral, for death seemed so close, and suddenly I realized how precious life was. All these years I've talked so flippantly of dying and now, confronted by the very specter of annihilation, I hung on to the sound of my breath, the sound of my heart pounding within me as if this pulse of animation held everything of any consequence and meaning for my future.

I'm sorry if I'm getting a little too melodramatic or emotional, but just be thankful that your Arden has lived to tell the tale. I know how this will shock and upset you (as it has for me), but such things are rather commonplace in a city of this size and I suspect that after not too many years and before too long, such events will be considered more typical than not. One must expect deranged and diseased individuals to suddenly decide to take as many other hardy souls along with them before they depart for their appointed place. (Up or down—we remain, as you have always led me to believe, sinners to the end.) I promise to be more careful and circumspect in the future and have therefore made a pact with myself to avoid subways and all other forms of mass transportation for the next few weeks, at the very least. You never can tell when this sort of nasty business will strike again.

Trust you are well and that your perennials are doing nicely. Remember me with affection to Aunt Violet. All my best and hoping to hear from you before too very long, I remain,

Your loving dutiful son(ny),

(Signed) Arden K. Hoffstetter

The neck to ankle chartreuse-shaded body shoved, elbows bent like the jutting wings of some powerful bird of prey, reminding him of that strange species of Australian aviform, the megapode *(Megapodius)*, whose habit it is to bury its eggs beneath mounds of decaying vegetation and rotting leaf piles. When the baby avian or megapodette hatches, it pushes its way up through the vegetable matter until it reaches the surface. Such was the analogy drawn by Arden K. when he saw Belinda running ahead of him, knocking aside other subway-goers in a mad rush of incredible purpose.

"Belinda! Belinda my baby! Wait for me! Why are you running away?" he called after her, the trail he was following leading him to the foot of an escalator which bridged the subway gap between the local and the express. He jockeyed for a position on the moving stairs, his eyes never leaving the constantly retreating figure of his friend. Both fleeing and fleeting, as it were. With no time for excuse-me's or other such formal displays of polite and expected behavior, he finally caught up to her.

"Why didn't you wait for me? What's the matter?" he asked.

"What's the matter?" with an hysterical laugh. "Nothing at all. Nary a thing. I just wanted to get some air, that's all."

"Are you all right? I was so terrified for you back there."

"Were you?" She cocked an eyebrow to one side, nearly losing her shoe as the escalator step upon which she was standing reached the top of its course. Together they stepped onto the platform maintained for uptown locals.

(These trains made stops at indeterminate numbered streets for people whose lives were not consumed by a morbid fear of being late, a morbid dread of simply taking their time.)

He went on, still quite overwrought, "I never thought

we'd get out of there alive or in one piece."

"Really," Belinda replied with the same expression of quizzical disbelief. "Don't you think you're exaggerating just a little? The rush hour isn't *that* bad."

Arden found his composure and level of tolerance rapidly diminishing. "What in God's name do you mean by that? We could have lost our lives. We could have been shot to smithereens. Doesn't that mean anything to you? Surely you saw that man fall right into my lap."

"What man?" with a look reserved only for viewing the insane and institutionalized.

"The man on the subway. On the train. One of the people who got shot. There were four shots, almost one right after another. Four bodies. What kind of game are you playing, anyway?"

"Are you sure you're all right, Arden? I mean, you do look a trifle peaked."

"I should hope so!" he shouted, and people turned around to watch, expecting movie cameras to emerge out of the tunnel's darkness at any moment. "A man went amuck!"

"Shhh, shhh," she whispered, patting him on the shoulder—much the Madonna and Child. "Everything will be all right in a minute. You just have to get hold of yourself."

"Stop whispering! *You're* the one who has to pull herself together, not me."

"But Arden, you had a little too much excitement today, that's all. Mr. Guysman must have terribly unnerved you, but please don't take it out on me, your friend."

"Mr. Guysman? Mr. Guysman!" he yelled back, refusing to accept or acknowledge her subtle suggestion that acetylsalicylic acid (otherwise known as aspirin) would do the trick. "Belinda, have you totally lost your senses? Do you mean to stand here and say that nothing happened down there when you know damn well that something did!" pointing to the lower level. "How can you dismiss all this by saying that I'm suffering from a headache?"

"But of course nothing happened," so sure of herself that he began to feel a gentle invasion of doubt creeping up behind him. "You must have been dreaming. You did seem a little shaky."

"Shaky! What do you mean of course I was *shaky*. A guy went daffy, batty, nutso and you're telling me not to shake. I think you have a helluva nerve expecting me to stand here and put up with *you*. In fact, I think that maybe it got to your head, too. I think maybe you're a little deranged yourself."

"Arden, keep talking like that and you can forget you ever had a friend named Belinda."

"Fuck all this trusty companion bullshit!"

"Look, child of woe, I don't have to stand here and listen to all this abuse. Everybody's staring at us like you're some kind of nut."

"Stop gritting your teeth as if I care what the masses have to say!"

"Okay, blow your cool. Make like a freak. Maybe you are a freak, Arden. Maybe you're . . ."

"But there was blood on my hand," he pleaded. "I felt it!" He looked down at his palm and stepped backwards, surprise catching him totally off balance, completely unprepared for what he saw. For his skin, aside from the usual amount of city dirt and grease, was unmarked, unblemished, mostly a natural fleshy pink. "I must have rubbed it off," he countered, his tone much lower, and the bystanders, disappointed and a little bored at not having gotten a chance to see a future Oscar-winner in action and on location, turned back to their gossip, newspapers, and best-selling potboilers.

"I just don't understand," he murmured.

"I think you were having acid flashes, baby," she snapped back. "And as for me, I'm going."

"But . . . but," he whimpered as the local train began to pull into the station. "I thought I'd take you for cocktails. I have a cocktail party I've been invited to. A really wonderful party. Really. It's just a few blocks from here."

"You forget: I have to see a man about a dog. Anyway, it's probably too late to do anything and tonight I happen to have a full schedule," she responded, evoking in his mind a shadowy picture of the Dark Lady of American Letters. "Thanks for everything and do try to calm yourself down. You'll only end up getting a heart attack or a stroke or something." With a vague wave of her hand she slipped into the moving crush of bodies.

"Sure," he mumbled, filled with seemingly endless despair.

But if she's going home she could have stayed on the Express until 86th Street, Hoffstetter realized as he watched the back of her jumpsuit pressed against the train's glass paneled sliding door. If nothing really happened, why was she in such a hurry to take the local? It just doesn't make sense.

Still perplexed, he let himself be pulled and carried along with the tide of early evening shoppers until, a few minutes later, he found himself thrust smack into twilight.

Chapter 5 ½

EDITOR'S NOTE: *Screen Confessions* magazine ran the following article just a few short months before it was forcedly suspended from further publication. The publisher is currently on extended vacation somewhere in the vicinity of the wilds of Brasilia and could not be reached for comment, but it is to their credit, and should be noted at this time, that *S.C.* was among the first of the periodicals and popular monthlies to recognize the emergence of Arden K. Hoffstetter as a unique force on the Hollywood scene and a herald of the beginnings of a brave new era in the history of the American film.

"SUDDENLY MY COLDS TURNED TO HOTS"—
How and Why Arden K. Hoffstetter Won the
Academy Award

In one glorious moment, on the night of April 14th of this year, the whole world changed for Arden Hoffstetter. Before that evening he had been just another of the hundreds of struggling new faces around Hollywood who had written a book to keep them busy. On that night, though, when our President predicted the results of the balloting and Arden won the Academy Award for the best male performance of the year in his film *Flush*, he stepped into a different class entirely. He jumped into the glittering arena of cinema greats.

The word around town, from the back lots and

commissaries of every studio to the posh meeting grounds of the stars, was that Arden would be a one-shot one-picture actor. They said he would be washed up before he ever got started and that he would be forgotten by the time the film was released. Already, the established members of this, the film capital of the world, were saying that his debut as an actor would be a devastating failure and the studio's worst mistake of the decade. Countless millions, not to mention the hopes and dreams of many, hung in the balance. But it seems that everyone figured this guy wrong. For Arden had courage, the kind of raw guts and nerve that makes stars out of mere men. He knew he could do it. He knew he could face up to the challenge and supreme test as few men could and with great courage he went out to prove his worth.

The role was difficult. Few leading men would have been willing to touch it. Yet it was this very difficulty and hardship which would prove, on that fateful night this past April, who had it when it really came down to the finish.

We spoke to Arden in his dressing room where he was enjoying an infrequent break. Busy at work in the film production of Jeremy Haberman's best-seller, *The Great American Novel*—in which he will play the lead as Tush Botwinick, a young man of considerable means who suffers at the hands of a beautiful but evil woman and a strange but neurotic uncle, Arden still found time to reminisce.

"Here," meaning Morgan City, Louisiana, where he was on location, "it's much easier to be yourself," he told us. "You don't have to put up with all the phonies and Gucci Groovies and in this business, let me tell you, there are plenty of those."

No wonder that word has gotten around the studio back lots and plush watering places of the stars, that Arden was an angry young man who minced neither gait nor words. How true!

"While I was working on *Flush*, playing the demanding but ultimately rewarding role of Telly, I was constantly on my guard and always on the defensive. I hadn't studied acting before taking the part. I only knew that if I, Arden Hoffstetter, could in some way *become* Telly, it would be right. Everyone was terribly helpful, but in the end, I had to go it alone. Frankly, I never for a minute doubted that I'd be nominated for the award. As soon as I saw the first day's rushes I knew I was golden. If you'll look back you'll note that just about every year someone's included in one of the two major acting categories who was billed in their picture as 'And Introducing.' It was 'And Introducing Arden K. Hoffstetter,' and I suppose that I was the best new introduction of the year."

A look of genuine sincerity shone on his interesting courage-filled face. Yes—candid and warm, gutsy and real, there were no two ways about our feelings when confronted by this honest expression of self-doubt.

"But I never expected to win the award. I mean, I was running against the greats—Dustin Hoffman, Mick Jagger, Richard Burton, and Woody Allen. I was the biggest dark horse there was. The tallest, too. So you can imagine my surprise when my name was called out. I nearly fainted I was so shocked and excited. I mean, I was just flabbergasted!"

What a surprise it must have been for this small-town Wisconsin boy! But Hollywood had once again proven that a person from humble beginnings, even with little talent, by working and struggling and giving their heart and courage while sleeping with the right people, could someday make it to the top.

"It was the most important day of my life, winning the Oscar and joining the ranks of movieland greats." He smiled.

What Arden does not talk about is his role as scriptwriter. Just imagine his disappointment when he failed to win his second Oscar! But, aside from this minor setback, the future seems to hold only sunshine and more bright lights. No youngster, Arden, already in his thirties, has been called by those in the know, "the Peter Ustinov of the sexy seventies." Within a few short months after the picture's release, Arden's name has been linked to every prominent and sexy young starlet in town. His appearance before the Senate Investigating Committee on National Morality, seen on coast-to-coast television by millions, has only earned him the applause of the entire industry. Indeed, what loyal video watcher can ever forget the fuzzy but impressive picture of Arden Hoffstetter jumping to his feet, putting his hand over his heart and declaring for all the nation to hear, "I stand for equal promiscuity for all, whether they be black, yellow, Puerto Rican, Jewish, or whatever."

We asked him about his friendship with Broadway actress Belinda Blumright and if there was any chance that the two of them would tie the knot before too very long.

"Belinda and I have been friends since my struggling Yorkville days when I was a nothing and she was just a dreamer. She's always been a great help to me in my career and I only wish her the best. I realize that Belinda must first think of her career and since we've been mostly friends, I seriously doubt if there's a proposal in the near or even distant future. But of course, I'm open to suggestions. In fact, I wanted her to play the role of Suzanne in this picture. It's the kind of gutsy part she seems to favor, but she had prior commitments to do an off-color revue in New York and had to beg off at the last minute. I think that when she finally does do a film, the *right* one for her of course, she'll end up becoming as big a star as I am. I've always had tremendous confidence in Belinda, you know, and I'm sure she'll get what she wants when the time is right for her."

Audiences around the world are still being electrified

seeing Arden go through his frenzied paces in *Flush*, and we here at *Screen Confessions* are equally confident that you fans out there will not be disappointed when you see him in his next no-holds-barred film-for-all. Some of the stills we had the privilege of viewing were just not to be believed! We have no doubt that Arden in *The Great American Novel* will once again set a high standard of excellence in courageous gutsy nudity in acting.

"At least the weather is hot and damp," he told us as his makeup man—the best that the producer's money could buy—came in to check out his local color. "When I was living up in New York I was always getting these bad winter colds, even in the summer," he laughed. "But here in the Deep South it seems that suddenly all my colds have turned to hots."

Chuckling uproariously, we thanked him for the time he had given us away from his busy schedule as well as this exclusive opportunity to hear his sincere and brave words. And needless to say, we'll be waiting impatiently to see this great man and brilliant actor come forth to win acclaim in all his future roles!

Yes, the screen is a far far brighter place these days thanks to improved lighting techniques and the hard work and know-how of men like Arden Hoffstetter.

Be sure to see Arden Hoffstetter's Oscar winning performance in Flush *for Donnie Bee Prods. He also stars in the soon-to-be-released motion picture,* The Great American Novel.

Chapter 6

He—the one we are most familiar with—stepped out onto Lexington Avenue (named after the subway line), right in front of Bloomingdale's the rather renowned department store of status labels. Immediately he found himself confronted by at least a score of young lisping lithesome men. At first he thought it was a streetside convocation of speech impedimenteurs. At second he thought it was an assemblage of deaf-mutes because of all the hands waving and flapping wildly at the air and at each other, but further observation led him to conclude that he had been thrust into a randomly assembled mini-culture which sometimes roamed the East Side streets. The men were all dressed in black, tops and bottoms alike, obviously still traumatized by the death of Judy Garland. Arden (whose own myth would put Esther Blodgett and Lily Mars to shame), the newly or at least recently established sexual landscapist, could not help admiring with a certain degree of amusement the prominence with which the youths displayed their thwarted virility: twenty or so similarly maintained outlines beneath the tight clinging cloth of their trousers. Realizing that someday codpieces would be the vogue, he flipped back in time for but an instant, saw the Ainu performing his act of studied Stanislavskian disrobing and decided that surely there must be exercises—yoga or isometrics—to increase and improve upon the length of things to come.

Determined not to allow the previous events of the day

to stand in the way of what promised to be clean wholesome fun, Arden then headed uptown, stopping at a small but reputable florist's to purchase a bunch of multicolored candytufts, thinking, as he fumbled for change, of the reception which awaited him at the home of the celebrated and inimitable Marchioness Mona Aikenclast.

The latter, unmarried but fruitful daughter of a wealthy indigo planter and known locally in all the better parts of town as the "Purple Prize," had recently been the winner of the $250,000 Grand Prize of the New York State Lottery. Money followed money, seeking its own level and in celebration of this unexpected but heavily taxed windfall, she was now entertaining nightly. Her salon, reputed to be the most stimulating in all of the city, and daily packed with promising hungry up-and-coming young artistic and artsy-craftsy talents, had caused one observant snip of a columnist to quip the now-famous catch phrase: "a little bit of Bloomsbury in ole New York."

So toward the Bloomsberries he now hurried, not yet creatively ripe but proud that Mona had picked him and had not forgotten to invite him to share in the beneficent good cheer and tomfoolery. But of course, for he was not heartless—seldom exhibiting those traits which bear witness to a weakness of character—he could not help but remain slightly distressed with the persistent vision of mass murder and congruent mayhem which still stained his air of thoughtful abandon. It was hard to play the role of master novelist, shoulders set above the crowd, with this indelible nightmare stamped upon his senses, so that an expression of indeterminate discomfort followed him up the brownstone steps of the Aikenclast town house where, from within, he recognized the most popular rock group of the day, the Manique Depressives, singing their all time oldie-but-goldie hit, "Don't Mess Up My Mind." Arden sang the words to himself:

SON OF THE GREAT AMERICAN NOVEL

Frodo was a fairy,
Hobbits such a bore.
Gandalf was a *schmuck*,
Though he knew the score.
And divinity, it reckons,
Beckons near and far.
Save the wicked child,
Spoil the distant star.

So don't mess up my mind, babe.
Don't mess up my head.
It's in bad shape as it is, babe.
My heart it's feelin' dead.

Then, humming politely and slightly off-key, he handed his frown to the butler and strode into the gaily-lit living room, gazing with introspective delight at:

waist-high pickled wood moldings

a buffet table set with sumptuous delicacies

a stuffed trochilus, obviously very expensive and recherché

a fireplace inlaid with precious woods from Cathay and environs

Mona ensconsed between two important-looking publisher types

a girl tucked into a corner, who,

as he moved closer, revealed herself with doll-like hand-painted china-blue eyes and chinaberry ("the yellow, berrylike fruit of the China tree") hair. Unmanicured bangs splayed across her forehead. Her skin was white, devoid of spirit, translucent as a soap shaving and stretched like a taut ache across her cheekbones. It all made him think—had she been pregnant—of someone suffering from an acute case of pre-parturient hysteria. Yet he said nothing. Without a drink in his hand, that fortifying pause that refreshes, he still felt too shy to delve into womb problems with a total stranger.

Leaving the two editors like bookends without

a volume to support, the Marchioness and undisputed patroness of the arts came forward, snatching a glass off a crowded tray, saying as she reached Arden's side, "I'm terribly distraught."

He leaned over and touched his lips to the dry powdered skin of her cheek. "You've never looked more ravishing, more intoxicating."

"Intoxica-ted, darling," she corrected, handing him the glass. "Drink this."

Bubbles rose to the top, burst, and split the surface one after another. "What is it?"

"A mimosa."

"The fruit of the tree?" wondering if when he put his lips to the glass the liquid, like its namesake, would shy away at his touch.

"Champagne and orange juice," she explained. "Nevertheless, I've just been informed by a reliable source that I'm suffering from iron-poor blood. Iron deficiency anemia, to be quite the medico. You probably have no idea what that means to a woman of my breeding and bearing. Think what it'll do to the pedigree," she went on in her characteristic voice which the same quipsome calumniator (dispenser of journalistic columns) noted and quoted above had recently referred to as "a cantorial Hadassah singsong."

"A pound of calf's liver twice daily should do the trick. Or try taking natures spelled backwards. But it's so good seeing you again."

"Yes, you have been away, haven't you." But her attention had strayed and the words slipped into a murmur. "If only we could do something for that poor child over there," and he followed her gaze to the frail young woman whose presence he had already been made painfully aware of. "So tragic, and so young."

"What's the matter with her?" deciding at the same time that he would have preferred to have seen grapefruit juice used instead of o.j.

"It'll just take hours," Mona sighed. "This should be a

happy time for you. A special time, don't you think?" and she winked naughtily like a blushing schoolgirl caught in the act.

Arden was surprised at her reticence. "After what I've already been through this evening, nothing else could shock me."

"Oh really? You haven't told me. Why, did you go somewhere?"

"An assignment," he said, proud to be part of the work force. "But what's wrong with the girl?"

"I'm afraid it's quite complicated, the least of which is that she thinks she's Rosemary's baby. Not the baby, not even Rosemary, but the whole book. Literary transference is what the doctors call it."

Hoffstetter looked over her décolleté shoulder at this huddled image of fright, wondering if the girl had just seen a Castevet. But her eyes, startlingly blue pinpoints, shone with an unhealthy Gothic terror and he knew— instantly as novelists sometimes do—that he had found suitable new material to help fill in the gaps of his masterwork.

Mona stepped back, obscuring the view, straightened herself up and placed her hands on his shoulders. "But you're looking splendid, splendid indeed. The very picture of imminent and rosy success. Someday you shall be a most eminent young man, Arden K. Hoffstetter, and I hope that you won't forget your old friend and admirer. I have an uncanny knack for picking out undiscovered talents. I see right through most people and the very first time I met you I said to myself, 'Mona dear, he's so inscrutable that he has to be the genuine article.' That's just what I told them. Those very words."

Arden shook his head and lowered his eyes to the parquet floor.

"Don't believe me," she laughed. "Wait. It'll all happen soon enough."

"The sooner the better. From your mouth to God's

ears, as certain segments of the population say, because I'm getting a little tired of waiting."

"Finish your book first, and then worry. If you weren't half as stubborn about not letting anyone take a peek..."

Arden raised his hand to her lips. "Please. You know we've gone over this before. I'd rather have a new script for this evening."

"Same as ever," she clucked her tongue. "Well, that's what happens when you get as old as I am. But come, there are people here I'm sure you're just dying to meet," and she led him off in search of new adventures.

Needless to say, so why say it, but the candytufts lay forgotten beneath their gaudy paper wrapping, tossed into a corner to mingle with the shadows and unseen tears.

Excerpts from: *The Mimosa Garden* or *Mona: The Early Memoirs of the Marchioness Mona Aikenclast*[1]:

It was at this time that the two of them first met, thanks, I may add, to my own little intervention, for had I left Arden to his own devices he would have been content to sit off to the side taking notes on all that was going on around him. Their devotion and mutual respect for each other manifested itself with surprising rapidity, tossing the two of them about on a veritable jetstream of creative and sympathetic emotion. Haberman enjoyed taking the upper hand, using the powers of his youth (although Arden was perhaps no more than five or six years his elder) to lead Hoffstetter forth into new fields and precious realms of singular experience. They would sit in the 'girl ghetto' singles bars, relishing the displays of quasi-nuptial behavior between the ribbon-clerks and touch-typists. Often they would venture down to the

[1]In the following passage it would appear that the Marchioness was indulging in a bit of unconscious plagiarism. She had obviously been reading *The Early Memoirs of Lady Ottoline Morrell*.

waterfront, to spend sordid muggy evenings in squalid seaside pubs, mixing with 'the masses' as Arden called them, or 'the people' as Haberman was wont to describe. Picking up strange friends and dangerous types, they amused themselves thusly, later peopling their novels with the individuals they had met during these exciting nighttime excursions into the nether world of sin and vice. And so great is the imitative urge which swells inside the human spirit that Arden took to altering his appearance to please the more eccentric and stylishly flamboyant Haberman. He began to wear his hair very long, like Lytton Strachey during his Augustus John period, and had one ear pierced, from which he sported a single shrimp or macaroni earring. He discarded his collars and velvet bow ties and wore only a rich purple (in homage to me, I would venture to say) scarf tied loosely around his neck, fastened with an Art Deco pin I had presented to him one summer afternoon at tea. They were, indeed, a most surprising and spirited pair as they walked the streets and avenues of up and downtown Manhattan.

I remember quite distinctly, having entered the event in my diary later that evening, the first day Arden was introduced to the young and charmingly effervescent Jeremy Haberman. He came to the door, strode into the living room and, seeing me in heated concourse with two gentlemen whose names defy remembrance, fell into my arms. He appeared to be on the verge of some catastrophic emotional and spiritual crisis, ill and bruised, nervous, hounded, and terribly shocked. I comforted him as best I could, trying to divert his attention and amuse him with childish trifles. It was only weeks later, after speaking one afternoon on the telephone to Haberman, that I discovered the terrible truth. To think that Arden could have gotten so emotionally involved with the lives of total strangers pleased me to a degree I found most annoying. But murder is a nasty business, and few who have partaken of the experience remain unmoved by it for many weeks to come.

Clever as he may have seemed to most, Arden Hoffstetter was nevertheless a troubled spirit. In the days before our unfortunate and most unpleasant altercation, of which I will reserve comment at this time, there were many unsettling moments when we were alone together. Often, a look of childish worry appeared upon his face, dampening and darkening the glow of radiant creativity which sprung forth from his eyes. He was one of that growing breed of individuals who torture themselves with uncertainties, constantly striving for what, in death, becomes an unreachable zenith of perfection. Although I admired his drive and his dedication to his art, I was constantly moved to remind him to be more gentle to himself—a phrase, I take it, which has been much quoted and overused these days. Whether he followed my suggestions or not, one will never know, but it is apparent in the body of work he will leave behind that his portraits, both written and cinematographic, will inspire countless others for generations yet to come.

"He was a most divine young man," said Roosevelt Geldinger, minutes after being introduced, and reminding Arden that his name was pronounced like the flower and not like the popular demagogue. "What did you think of it?"

"The murder or your book?" Arden replied, staunchly repelled with unequivocal fervor from this smug little man whose sensational best-seller, *With Malicious Spite*, had propelled him into the ranks of the beautiful and talked about people. Few could ever say, "It left me cold," after reading this graphic non-fiction novel. With disquieting ease and fingertip facility, Geldinger had written the story of a handsome young man who had systematically raped and murdered five airline steward-esses in a crowded luxury apartment in the high-rent district of Manhattan's upper East Side. Written as if he were taking on-the-spot notes, hidden perhaps under one of the beds, Geldinger later had a much publicized jail-cell osculation with the killer which culminated in a farewell dinner before he went to the electric chair. *Life* and *Look* each devoted an entire issue, with many full-page color photos, to this final tryst which had been—at Geldinger's insistence and expense—catered by an eminent French chef and this had, in turn, greatly increased the sales of the paperback edition. Although some of today's outspoken youth had leveled an attack of coldbloodedness against the author, few of the older and more established critics had dared to say a word against the work. Thus, with a well-funded publicity and advertising campaign containing most of McLuhan's messages, Roosevelt Geldinger had made enough of a bundle to be able to court the rich and famous with unexcelled alacrity. Indeed, his Pajama Party in the (then) ruins of the Astor Hotel was a social event which attracted all those individuals who made a point of getting on the cover of *Time* magazine. Everything was done with gusto, excess, and an eye for color. It was said that the dress designers made fantastic profits that year, outdoing themselves as they went about exploring new ways to fashion elegant pajama outfits, all fantastically overpriced *couturier* originals which were soon copied with union labor and cheaper materials and sold in bargain basements throughout the nation, thereby stemming an imminent recession which might have severely crippled the economy.

"The novel of course," Geldinger went on from where we had left off so abruptly.

Arden, who had his hands full with a crust of rye on which he had carelessly overloaded the black dyed eggs of the Iranian lumpfish, thought for a moment before stating with a noncommittal monotone, "It was interesting. It held my attention. But frankly, if you don't mind my saying so, I find your earlier fiction much more lyrical and less commercial."

Geldinger stiffened. "I don't believe I've read anything of yours," the little man said sharply, digging a well-suited custom mohair elbow into the nearest of his fawning companions.

Someone giggled nervously and a lady wearing a dress that looked like it was in need of a transfusion excused herself for air.

"No one has. I still have about five hundred pages to go."

Geldinger let out a sharp birdlike laugh. "I daresay that's a novel in itself. How much have you written so far, if I may be so bold?"

"You may," Arden condescended, continuing, "Roughly twenty-five hundred pages. A little more or a little less."

"Index cards, did you say?" with a most piercing rising inflection.

"Pages," Arden repeated, accustomed to rudeness from those who were ultimately unsure of themselves.

"Pages?" Roosevelt said aloud, for, like most of us, this friend and confidant of a national widow was impressed by length in all things. In fact, behind his back his closest closet friends were apt to refer to him as "Rosie the Size Queen." *"Tu es,"* reverting to the uncalled for familiar with which he was most comfortable, *"un nouvel Tolstoy, monsieur, n'est-ce pas?"*

Arden, who had also read *The Magic Mountain,* countered with, *"Mais oui, et mes amis pensent que je suis un homme grand."*

"Your syntax is off, *mon drôle d'ami. Mais je me tiens trop mal,* as most uneducated people say, though I'd certainly be most curious to see what you've done. Is it as great a book as mine?" Although he had meant the last to sound sarcastic, Arden was able to detect in Geldinger's speech an undercurrent of competitive *mal d'esprit.*

"I'm afraid that depends on one's definition of great."

"An interesting point," as the circle of listeners reduced

the clinking of their mimosa glasses to a minimum, tightening around this thickening repartee. "What then, is *your* definition of greatness in literature?"

Arden had discussed this with a number of his friends and was at no loss to explain. "As far as I'm concerned, a great novel must succeed on three primary levels. On the first level it must be entertaining. The reading of it must be an enjoyable experience—even if the reader suffers emotionally, he still is involved with characters and situations. If the book is plotless, then the prose must be of such brilliance as to make up for the lack of rudimentary eventfulness.

"For example, I'd say that *Finnegans Wake* does not succeed as a work of great literature, whereas *Ulysses* most certainly does. The lay reader, or even the above-average reader, cannot be made to follow Joyce's complexities with any serious degree of understanding. There are too many private allusions and word games which have meaning only for the author. Therefore, as literature, I'd say that the novel fails because, as we all well know, art must communicate. If a work of literature fails to communicate it has not succeeded on this primary level."

"But is not this qualification rather subjective? Surely there must be people, even a goodly number, who were able to read and enjoy say, *Finnegans Wake*, and found that it communicated with them," the published author replied.

"Taste is always subjective. When I say 'communicate' I should preface that by explaining that I mean the reading public, but not necessarily the Joe Average reader. There *is* a difference, you know. I'm talking about communicating to someone who doesn't read trash, but also someone who hardly ever picks up what professors like to call a 'classic'. That means not only those who read to escape, using the printed word as a narcotic, but also those who read to learn and, as a popular generality, broaden their scope."

"Then what constitutes your second criterion?" Geldinger asked, his facial expression losing some of its initial conceit as he grew more interested.

"At this point the definition becomes even more difficult to pin down. For, on a secondary level, a great work must be of such thematic significance that the reader will be able to draw parallels with his own life, applying lessons he has learned to the world around him, the world which confronts him on a day-to-day basis. You see, a great book is not limited by era or geographic location. It is, within itself and the universe it re-creates, structurally timeless.

"And on a tertiary level," Arden continued, surprised that he had not been interrupted, "the stability of the definition collapses completely. For we move from a level of assumed objectivity—assuming that we agree on what constitutes enjoyment and communication—to one of purely subjective criticism. For, on this third level, a great work must possess that indefinable quality which cannot be put into words, but which we all know is there. This, I'd think, includes the inherent beauty of its prose, its construction, its mastery of theme and language, character, insight, development. In other words, all those things which give a great work its fundamental symmetry of design and unity of purpose."

"And who, in your estimation, has succeeded in writing great works of literature?"

"Whoever wrote the Bible."

The audience relaxed, prepared as they were for one of Geldinger's more usual party tactics: the verbal whiplashing and final disgrace. "Go on."

"Perhaps Hesse and Mann. Most assuredly Tolstoy and Dostoyevsky. Those just for starters."

"And who do you think in this country is writing great literature these days?"

"Only Nabokov. There are some fine contemporary

156

writers, but I don't think very much, if any, of their work will be remembered a hundred years from now, except perhaps as an obscure kind of period piece or a curio from a bygone age. But I think that Nabokov will. Probably because he seems to me to come closest to fulfilling the three canons I've already mentioned." His throat was now parched to the extreme and for the first time he realized how many people had gathered around them to listen, wondering how he had gotten off on such a long and convoluted tangent. Feeling shy, he looked around for Mona to extricate him from his fears.

"One more thing," said Roosevelt Geldinger. "Is *your* novel great, Mr. Hoffstetter?"

Arden turned his head back. "I've already given it five years of my life, but I'm probably my own worst critic. I think it's good, at least I *hope* it's good, even on the days when I'm assailed with terrible doubts. But it will be up to the reading public to decide on its final worth."

"And not the critics?" asked an unseen voice at the edge of the confab.

"A great book is read by people," Arden replied, straining to match the voice with the unglimpsed face. "They are the ones who must make the final judgment. Too many books are loved and adored by the critics, but find themselves all too often quickly relegated to the pedant's shelf. And if they decide to resurrect my literary worth and artistic standing fifty or a hundred years from now, I probably won't even be around to care."

"Arden, I must say that I have found our little chat rather disquieting. It gives me much to think about, even more to ponder at my leisure," Geldinger spoke again, his eyes resting below the Hoffstetter belt level. "Perhaps you will be my guest sometime and we can go into this at greater length."

Greater length, Arden repeated to himself, nodding his head with wary appreciation.

"I see you're doing beautifully," Mona whispered, coming up from behind him to steal a hand into his trouser pocket. "You've obviously passed the first test."

Everyone is goosing my life away, our author thought, enjoying at the same time the attention being paid to his pleasure parts.

At which point the previously unseen face caught up with its voice as a young man stepped forward. He was a thinnish young man who carried himself with a swagger of insecurity, perhaps feeling that the world viewed him as fatter and less trim than he really was.

"Arden my love, let me introduce you to a fellow traveler," Mona interjected brightly, urging the newcomer forward and into the light. "This is Jeremy Haberman, a most charming and talented young man."

This charming and most talented young man was a Scorpio, and a double one at that. As such (even with an Aquarius rising sign), he found that his life was controlled by his genitals, his thoughts centering on the creative use of his life-making apparatus. He had often sought to master the whims of fleeting but sudden erections and now took to wearing long Edwardian cut jackets to conceal the actions of muscles which were not regulated by conscious thought. For this reason and others, he placed considerable import upon his appearance and had, over the last few years of struggling but dedicated maturity, catalogued those resemblances which others had discovered, so that:

when he wore glasses, on those infrequent occasions when his contact lenses were either lost or troublesome, he had been told he looked like a cross between John Lennon and Woody Allen

fresh from the hair stylist he had a Warren Beatty windswept quality about him

from afar people mistook him for someone they either thought they should know or thought they had seen on the Johnny Carson show a few nights before

close up they said he reminded them of a British actor whose name and pederastic ambience had escaped the moment his mother would often say with delight, 'Who is this gorgeous young man? My son? Where does he get such exquisite taste he looks like such a real movie star?'

No one had ever told him that he looked like himself, like Jeremy Haberman the author of *The Great American Novel*, which may or may not account for his rather disjointed picture of himself in his own eyes and the eyes of those around him.

"Jeremy who?" Arden asked, wheels turning and assorted mechanisms and gears clicking into recollection.

"Haberman," the fashionably dressed youth repeated, standing nervously with his hands behind his back and hoping that he was making a good first impression. "Have we met before? I really don't recall," he recited the lines he had been instructed to say. "Actually, I've led a very sheltered life."

Arden wondered where he had heard that line before. He started to say something, changed his mind and declared, "Only on the printed page." He pumped the boy's hand vigorously. "I only just had the pleasure of reading your novel."

Haberman's eyes widened until they seemed to fill his face—a look and phrase made popular by lady writers. "Tush Botwinick and his gang?"

"The very same. It was devastating, just brilliant."

"Oh . . . wow! Are you an editor? They didn't tell me you were an editor. Are they going to publish it? Oh, wow, let me sit down! This is just too much of a coincidence!" And with a great display of exclamatory dramatics, he fell gracefully into the nearest chaise lounge.

"I'll leave you two youngsters alone to discuss your art." Mona excused herself, the train of her silk hostess gown reminding Arden, as she exited, of the bedraggled tail-feathers of a peacock spurned.

Turning his attention once again to the young and eager unlined face which awaited his every breath, Arden intuitively recognized the first shapeless moments of a new-found friendship and he smiled, relaxed and serenely responsive to the needs of another.

Viewed from across the room they appear rigid, frozen attitudes of party sculpture, as we take a station break to digress . . . as is our pleasure. We will leave them this way for a moment, perhaps just to get better acquainted with a certain degree of privacy (secluded from the watchful reader's eye), perhaps for Arden to explain his role as free-lance reader and not editor, so that when we return, they will have dispensed with the boring necessities of introductory chitchat and may go on to matters which are (we venture to guess) both sacred and profane.

Once upon a time, in the Fifties when things were less expensive, when payola was the rage but it was harder to be yourself and say what you really felt, a young fellow by the name of Arden K. Hoffstetter was growing up, not at all absurd. Inch by inch he was outgrowing his Doctor Dentons and denim Play-togs here in this rustic rural corner, this "nap's-worth" of the American Dream.

While his peers were busy saying, "See ya later, alligator," listening to Elvis Presley and holding their noses with two fingers to the tune of "he who smelt it dealt it," Arden Hoffstetter was busy laying away plans for his future.

"What do you want to be, Arden dear?" asks his mother one spotlessly kitchen clean afternoon as he sits in the back yard burying his nose in a copy of *Memoirs of Hecate County*, thoroughly pleased that he is able to enjoy an experience which has been denied the residents of the State of New York, where its sale is prohibited.

"I want to be happy," he says without looking up.

"I mean what do you want to *do* with your life, dear. The whole world is open to you and everything is at your disposal. You have every opportunity right at your fingertips, just for the asking. You can do things that those who are more unfortunate than us cannot."

"Name one."

"One what?"

"One unfortunate," says the stubborn cynical young Arden.

"Why, Essie Cannon's little boy is a colored child and you know that he'll never be a success unless he becomes a singer or a tap dancer with his innate sense of rhythm," Mrs. Hoffstetter explains with patient provincialism. "I'm just curious, Arden, that's all."

"I want to be famous. And rich. And fall in love with someone who will be quite selfless, who will end up losing her own identity, who will care about me more than I care about myself. And who, in the end, will die by her own hand if I happen to die first."

"What morbid thoughts you have for someone so young and impressionable," his mother says, shaking her head in time to the meter of her words. "They certainly don't come from my side of the family."

"Nor do they come from father's, for I am a romantic, incurably so," replies her only son, his fingers busy turning to another controversial page.

"Well, you certainly can't go through life romanticizing," she reminds him, leaning over his shoulder to find out what he is reading so intently.

"And why not?"

"Because... because fantasizing doesn't pay the bills, dear. Why can't you be a little more practical and realistic, like your father was?"

"The artist is above realism, above explanation or practicality," trying, at the same time, to recall where he had culled this late Victorian epigram.

Blossom Hoffstetter sighs and absently twists a lock of hair around her finger. "I didn't know you wanted to be a painter, Arden. You should be taking lessons or something constructive like that."

"A writer, mother. I'm going to be a world-famous writer, a student of manners and mores, morals and morality. Right now I'm still in the planning and observing stage, taking mental notes on the behavior of everyone around me."

"Arden!" and she is quite shocked. "You haven't been poking your nose behind locked doors, have you?"

"Mother," he consoles her, laying his hand in her lap.

"Or looking over garden walls or into open windows," she continues with considerable alarm. "Have you, Arden?"

"No," he laughs, finally putting down his book on the grass so that his mother can at last take a look at the title and the rather lurid three-tone drawing which has nothing whatever to do with the plot or contents.

"Sometimes I just don't understand you, son. You want so much more than anyone else. I only hope that someday you'll catch up to all your dreams," she tells him with quiet maternal solace.

"Everything takes time, mother. Time and patience and hard work. I'll make it. I have to, because I'm basically a kind person."

Thinking that kindness has nothing to do with it she kisses him on top of his forehead, gets to her feet and smoothes out her dress. He doesn't look back as the screen door slams behind her retreating footsteps, but stares down at the cover of the book and tries to imagine what words it would take to produce a fictional orgasm.

An independent testing laboratory would have concluded, after seeing Arden and Jeremy in heated concourse amidst the Aikenclast retinue, that these two gentlemen had known each other far longer than revealed by an actual tabulation of minutes. So quickly were they drawn together, kindred spirits cast from similar life-molds, that they soon became oblivious to the comings and goings of Mona's sycophantic entourage. There was much to discuss and each, not accustomed to being on the listening end, found it difficult to keep still.

Mona herself was quite delighted to have proven to be the catalytic force behind their introductory meeting and she hovered by the chaise lounge, forever signaling for fresh drinks and assorted hors d'oeuvres, both hot and cold. It should be mentioned at this point that the Haberman palate ran toward smoked salmon, guacamole, and *pâté de foie gras aux truffes*, whereas Hoffstetter was more inclined to beluga caviar—the larger the grain the more to his liking—fresh oysters and, weather permitting, *quiche Lorraine*.

"I really don't see what's so funny about it," Arden went on as we zero in for a close-up. "I think that playing the lead in the movie version of my novel would be an extraordinary experience. Just think of all the new material I'll get for my next book."

"Are you a writer or an actor?" Jeremy replied, his mouth filled with Mona's hand-picked morsels.

"Why, I can be anything I want to be, once I've set my mind to it. I've told you all about my theory of the media. . . ."

"It's all very well, but I would think that when one gets too close to their work, they lose all the necessary objectivity. I'm rather content to slug out life at my typewriter, if you know what I mean. I have some great ideas still in the planning stage. A book reworking the Oedipal myth called *Mother Fucker*, and something about a tumultuous journey on the Staten Island ferry in search of self. . . ."

"It's been done," Arden said glumly, rather unnerved by all of Haberman's youthful ambitiousness. If only I can finish *Flush*, he thought to himself. But the end keeps eluding me, as if there's nothing left to write about.

"There's so much to write about," Jeremy told him, unknowingly psychic in his reply. "I'll never stop!"

"Name one."

"One what?" Playing the same game Hoffstetter's

mother had played years before.

"One thing to write about that hasn't been done yet. I'm at a loss for new material. There was a strange looking girl here earlier, but she seems to have disappeared. She'd have probably been very interesting for a nice neat incisive character study."

"Did she have blondish hair?" Haberman asked, pulling out a hanky from his back pocket and wiping off each finger in turn.

"Yellowish, like thatch, and marvelous haunted blue eyes."

Haberman jumped to his feet. "We still have time!" he said with great alarm, knowing that his timing had been perfect.

"Sit down," replied Arden, to whom any great display of emotion was most disconcerting. "Explain yourself."

"She must be on her way to Z's. Oh, I hoped it wouldn't have to come to this and now it may be too late."

"Too late for what?"

"How long ago was it that you last saw her?" Haberman went on impatiently.

"She was sitting in a corner about an hour ago. Maybe a little longer. But who the hell is Z?"

Haberman looked at him unbelievingly. "You mean you don't know?"

"No."

"You haven't heard?"

"No."

"Are you sure?"

"Of course I'm sure. Who is he?"

"It's a pretentious literary trap, one of the most diabolical of this or any other season. For he's more than likely the most insidious member of the medical profession left in the city. Not even the chiropractors will claim him for their own. But are you coming with me, or are you just going to sit there and let life pass you by?"

"I'll not be called an Oblomov," Arden K. replied defensively.

"Look, I thought you were in such great need of new material. This'll be the perfect opportunity."

"Frankly, I don't know what you're going on about. But if it'll make things any easier, I'm with you," and he rose from his place and tidied up the wrinkles in his trousers. "Shouldn't we thank Mona before we go?" he asked as he followed his new friend toward the front door even as a dozen new faces came in off the street.

"There isn't any time, Every second . . ."

"Is precious."

"I really don't think that was called for," Haberman shot back. "There's no reason why we have to start working against each other. And as for Mona, though I expect she'll pop up when we least expect her—just write her a note tomorrow. She'll treasure that more and years from now it might even be worth a small fortune."

The butler had misplaced Hoffstetter's frown, but as he thought he would have no need for it, the present company being so agreeable, he had the servant promise to send it over to Yorkville first thing in the morning should it happen to turn up. Once outside, he walked cheerfully and looked rather encouraged and lightheaded in his brown-velvet bow tie and jaunty patent leather step. Alas, alack, poor Arden K. If only he had retained a handy-dandy and ready scowl, if only he had had but a single premonition of impending disaster.

But he hadn't, and that is precisely the stuff of novels.

Chapter 6½

ONE WOULD think, after faithfully and lovingly following our narrative up to this point, that the road to Arden K. Hoffstetter's success was not fraught with difficulties, setbacks, or other such annoying hindrances. Actually, it was not as easy as that. Not nearly. After Arden completed *Flush* he went through a period of slightly more than twelve months when the doors to his eventual fame and mass popularity appeared to be forever barred. Years later, he would call this time the "Dingy Days," and it was a rare occasion when he would ever discuss them. Although he soon enough commenced work on his second novel, *Spit*, one far less grandiose in scope and more intimate in tone and concept, and one which would earn him additional praise, it is amazing for us (in this genocidal day and age) to discover how many people ignored his work, blinded as they were to any of the simple rudiments of literary taste. For those of you out there who have suffered similarly, at the ends of similar ignoramuses, it gives us great pleasure to reproduce just a small sampling of letters from literary agents—or shall we say without subtlety, literary impostors—which can be found in the files of the Hoffstetter Archives, now in possession of the Society Library of New York.

September 29, 197—

Dear Mr. Hoffstetter:
Thank you for letting us read *Flush*.

I'm sorry to confess that I have made several attempts to read this book and found I did not understand it enough to really get into it. So I know you can only consider that I am entirely stupid and I will unhappily condescend to agree. Undoubtedly, another agent will feel quite differently about it but it is not for us, having more than slightly offended our sensibilities. I doubt if we could even interest Grove Press, so I return it to you forthwith under separate cover with real regret.

Sincerely,
[signed] Patricia Mae Squire

November 18, 197—

Dear Mr. Hoffstetter:

Your manuscript *Flush* arrived today, somewhat the worse for its trip. (See enclosed part of wrapper.) The sides of the three boxes were torn off, and many of the pages were out of order. The title page and two following pages (Is the single-spaced page with the paragraph beginning "The water was dotted..." and ending "....'Compositions' on the cover" the third page of the manuscript?), as well as pages 3–57, are dog-eared. The rest of the pages, assuming that none are missing and that page 2973 is the last page, are in good enough condition to warrant my attention, although I am still somewhat disturbed that your type face is so small.

I wish you'd check our address; we haven't been at 50 Rockefeller Plaza for over two years, not since my wife's mother died and we were forced to find more reasonable accommodations. I don't know whether or not the fact that your manuscript was sent to an old address is in any part responsible for the condition in which it arrived, but I think it's a good idea to insure manuscripts that are mailed.

I'll be looking forward to reading *Flush*. I would appreciate it if you would send us enough postage to cover its return, insured for $100.00, which would be about $3.50. Also, if a cover letter accompanied the manuscript, please send me a copy, as none arrived with it. I also must know whether or not the book has been submitted to any publishers, and if so, which ones.

Thank you for sending us the novel. I'll be looking forward to hearing from you.

Sincerely yours,
[signed] Selig J. Manning

January 7, 197—

Dear Mr. Hoffstetter:

I'm sorry it's taking so long to get to *Flush*, but we have quite a backlog. I did read a couple of chapters shortly after receiving your November 29 letter. (Thanks for the letter and the $3.50 return postage, by the way.) I try to make a practice of doing this when I don't expect to be able to get to a manuscript for some time, because I think it's unfair to a writer to hold up his work for a long time if it's going to turn out to be way out of line.

Yours is good enough—to judge by the start you've made—to warrant our keeping it for a complete reading. I must say that the bulk of the work seems impressive, to judge by the sheer volume and output alone. I appreciate your patience, and promise that I'll read the rest of the book before too much longer.

Best wishes,

Cordially,
[signed] Selig J. Manning

February 23, 197—

Dear Mr. Hoffstetter:

I'm sorry not to have an encouraging report on *Flush* for you. There are some good satirical touches in it, but I couldn't sense any plot. I was aware of far too much dialogue and description, a morbid approach to man's sexual and technological foibles, and too little action. That is, too little that seemed to be happening to the characters. Frankly, I particularly couldn't understand Telly, and found him, on a superficial level, to be a rather indolent and oppressive kind of hero, as well as suffering from a warped view of the world around him.

I can be wrong, of course. If you feel strongly enough about it, you should try publishers and other agents. Have you thought about the possibility of using a Vanity Press? If you have any money to invest in your work, this would seem to me to be the surest way to get your novel published.

I'm very sorry to have taken so long to read the manuscript which was a mammoth effort on my part, and want to thank you for your patience and understanding.

Best of luck.

Cordially yours,
[signed] Selig J. Manning

August 27, 197—

Dear Mr. Hoffstetter:

You have been most patient in allowing me to keep your manuscript all these months without once telephoning me about it. Mr. Habeman (sp.?) phoned me yesterday to inquire and I do feel guilty for having held the novel so long. But Mrs. Ranchson and I have just finished reading *Flush*, spending two entire weekends at the task and, while we are both very much impressed by the brilliance and versatility of your writing, we both agree that the novel itself is not entirely a success. I am afraid I have decided not to take it on for submission, as I do sincerely doubt I could interest a publisher in it. The sheer volume of your "epic" would, I think, discourage its publication as a working commercial venture, as the taste of today's reading public runs to considerably lighter stuff. I know, of course, that any discerning publisher would be interested in your potential as a writer, for it is clear that you are an enormously gifted one.

Shall I hold the manuscript of the novel for your pick-up or would you like me to mail it back to you? The former method would save you the considerable postage costs involved, I may add.

The best of luck and again, my apologies for the delay.

Sincerely,
Jeff H. Ranchson
(dictated by him and signed in his absence per V.R.)

P.S. Perhaps you might try your hand at novelettes or Gothics. They might meet with greater success on today's difficult and competitive market.

JHR

Chapter 7

Aware of human imperfections, ready to accept the games that people played, even willing to try to understand a scene that was alien to his own nature, Arden K. suppressed his fear and growing distrust and sat on his metaphorical fence, hoping for the best, but, at the same time, ready to jump each way at a moment's notice.

They were in a taxi heading south, the driver complaining with customary bitchiness that he never heard of no Patchin Place, and give a working man a break, I was on my way back to the garage and I haven't even had my dinner yet.

Haberman slid the glass partition along its track, sealing off the front seat words, the palm of his hand moist with nervous anxiety because he had failed—despite his mother's repeated warning—to use a man's deodorant. He leaned back in the seat, fumbled in his jacket for a cigarette which he lit and inhaled as if he were preparing for his end, or at least, his final journey.

"You know why they put up these glass enclosures between passenger and driver?" he asked Arden K., not waiting for a reply. "Because it protects us from mealymouthed cabbies who don't want to do their job."

The driver, despite the barrier, heard everything and replied, "Listen Bud. If you don't like the service I can drop you off at the next corner."

"Why don't you shut up and watch where you're driving," Jeremy snarled, feeling his oats and safety because he was out of reach of the man's angry grasp. "I didn't ask for a soliloquy."

"Take it easy," Arden whispered with embarrassment. "He's only human. It's not worth getting so excited about."

"Who's excited?" Haberman laughed. "He just lost his tip, that's all."

"Then do me a favor and cool it. There's enough going on without you having to add to it."

At this, Jeremy flashed him a tossing look of exasperation and Arden felt like a child who is unable to comprehend the bitter short-tempered antics of his elders and betters. He stared straight ahead, the lights along Lexington Avenue, red to green and back again, distorted through the two sheets of glass.

I'm like a retard, he thought, letting myself be dragged like a freak from place to place without mouthing a word of protest. Patchin Place? I don't even know where in God's name he's taking me.

It would not be a source of consolation or even inspiration for us to tell him. How sorry we are that we cannot whisper words of endearing encouragement into his ear, soothing airs of confidential compassion. Of course, knowing all, seeing beyond the borders of mortal sight in our atemporal artistic plane, we stop to wonder if Jeremy Haberman is as altruistic as he appears to be. For we see that the images contained within the stuccoed house on Patchin Place, cascading voluptuously along the walls and polished floors, and bared months later by a special task force from the D.A.'s office, seem to hold only visionary glimpses into a world made popular by smut peddlers habituating the Times Square area of midtown Manhattan.

"Do you have a woman?" Haberman asked, the cigarette dangling gangsterlike from the corner of his mouth, set between a pair of full sensual lips whose genetic and ethnic origins the young man had tried— rather unsuccessfully—to hide for years.

"Not on a permanent basis. I live alone."

"At your age?" he replied, much amazed. "You're sure now that you don't like boys?" he went on with a self-satisfied laugh.

Arden was put off by such smugness. "No, it's not my scene, and yes, at my age I live alone. In fact, I like living alone. I like the freedom. Any more questions?"

"It's just disappointing, that's all."

"What is?"

"Nothing. Just forget it. Everyone's ready to jump down your throat. Don't get so hostile, man. I'm only trying to do you a favor."

"Why?" asked Arden K., sullen and angry and asserting his independence.

"Because they told me all about you and it sort of caught my fancy."

"Oh they did, did they?" Arden said sarcastically, not knowing what the boy was really talking about. "How very nice for you."

"Yes and no. Depends on how you look at it. Anyway, you're my friend and I like to help my friends out of jams."

"But you only know me a couple of hours. At the most. And what kind of jam are you talking about? I never said I was in any trouble."

"But you are. Just look at yourself. You're sitting on the biggest splash in publishing history since the astronauts wrote their book accusing NASA of turning them into emotionless machines. But you don't have an ending. You're not inspired. You feel dried up, just like they did. Wired up in space so they couldn't jerk off for fear the doctors back on earth would know what was going on up there. *Kaput*. Finished."

"Hold on now," Arden cautioned. "Let's not get too personal. I never asked for a favor and I never asked for an ending."

Haberman put his hand to the door even though the cab was still in motion. "Do you want me to leave?" he asked without any intention of stepping outside. "If you're unhappy about everything you can go back home. To your books and your typewriter, if you call that living. Here I am, going out of my way, doing a good turn and taking you to Z's for what will probably be the most eye-opening experience of your life, more than likely destined to change your whole literary style, and you're giving me a hard time. Arden, I don't need this kind of aggravation. I have enough of my own. Up to here," and he drew his hand across his throat as a measure of his lack of patience. "I knew I shouldn't have gotten involved."

"I'm the one who got himself involved, not you," Arden said. "But I just wish you'd be a little more explicit about Z. And what did that girl have to do with this, anyway?"

Questions, they're always asking questions," rolling his eyes up as if heaven would give him the strength and courage to go on. "That chick happens to be the key to my salvation."

"Now I've heard everything!"

"Okay, don't believe me. I only wish I could tell you more, but I don't know you long enough," Haberman continued, turning his head in Arden's direction. "Besides, my parents are still alive."

What does that have to do with anything? Hoffstetter wondered, also puzzled by the meaning of Jeremy's intent stare. After a few seconds, feeling uncomfortable and guilty for no apparent reason, he turned his eyes away and redirected his attention to the scene beyond the car window. The cab stopped for a light and at the corner he saw an old woman, old and white and wrinkled like everybody's grandmother, bent over a litter basket, retrieving with her liver-spotted fingers empty soda pop bottles, returnables which she deposited in a torn brown shopping bag as creased and brittle as her skin. She wore the already overloaded bag around her wrist along with an odd assortment of India rubber bands and similar elastics.

But he had no time to dwell on the scene, dismissing it

as just another part of the America he both loved and hated. His mind was too involved with questions whose answers would only make his friend unhappy. He wanted to apologize to his companion, but the moment was gone, lost as the cab picked up speed, and Arden was left with embarrassment and unvoiced compassion coating his tongue like some doctor's nostrum.

He muttered awkwardly, "Some can and some can't."

"What?"

"Nothing," Arden murmured, wanting to reach over and touch him on the shoulder as an older brother might pat his sibling rival, but certain that in the light of recent unspoken insights such a display of confidence would only have been immediately and gratefully misinterpreted.

We exist on a sexual landscape, he recited to himself, but why in the world must it always lead to hassles? Why can't things be nice and easy?

In an age when men were exploring the landscapes of the Moon, Arden K. often felt like an unmanned spacecraft hurtling through the vast microcosmic reaches of his unconscious. He saw himself as a computer existing in a vacuum, programmed in this atomless space where no emotions penetrated. Then he would grow unhappy, start to feel sorry for himself and the image would go nova, disintegrating as it rocketed into the gravitational pull of the sun.

Or else he conceived of living within the script of a panoramic psychodrama, his role as yet undefined, enacting movements of his limbs and organs to please the whims of the psychomaster, the unseen One who watched his every move. Then he would start to laugh at himself, or stop to look at his face in a piece of looking glass, and the thoughts would congeal in such a way that he was able to spit them out, like a glob of mucus tossed casually into the gutter.

He was not afraid of fines and city ordinances, and he knew it was an "ego trip" to put himself above the level of the crowd, to look down with amused detachment at the actions of those around him. He was not cynical, but he was unmoved and uninvolved. He watched the students fighting to win their rights, sympathized with them, but said nothing. He listened to the Black Nationalists, was proud that they were rediscovering their heritage, but could not find the time to read their works or see their plays or listen to their music. He opposed the war in Vietnam, but never marched, never even wore a protest button, always finding adequate excuses on rally days— prior engagements and commitments at home and with himself—to prevent him from declaring his anti-war beliefs.

He loved quickly, effortlessly, preferring girls in their early twenties who had recently left their mothers and were only staying in Big City for the present and not the future, a week or month at most before they ventured on to other places: usually Europe, San Francisco, or to a college friend in Boston. He sometimes wondered why he could not love anyone who was not a transient, a here-and-there person living a day-to-day existence. He wondered, but he did not change his ways.

Perhaps, although it is only a guess, a calculated hypothesis, but perhaps Arden K. was simply—how cunning and devious are the *simple* words of man!— afraid, scared of jumping off the fence. Being frightened, he grew self-satisfied and came to think of his precarious position as a favored one, a better way, the only natural choice for a man of independent spirit.

Why have we stopped to dwell on such interior matters? Because, now, heading in the direction of Greenwich Village in a yellow taxi cab with a grumpy driver, Arden was unaware that his past was catching up to him, that the moment of understanding was approaching when he would be called upon to make unalterable decisions. For in the search for the perfect ending to his novel, he would find an answer to the unfinished ending he had inserted in his soul.

It was a mews street, a muse street, an amusing and charming alleyway amidst the glass boxes of the new-moneyed. It was a stucco house, a town house, a carriage house with ivy scaling along the rough hewn walls. There was a brass knocker on the door which bore the shape of a dog's head, *alto-rilievo* with fangs bared and scowling eyes. There was a knot in the wood which bore the imprint of a paw, a canine paw subtly etched with master craftsmanship. Arden sensed adventure, and adrenalin pumped into his bloodstream, giving him courage, conviction, added endurance and temporary relief.

"Knock," Haberman directed him, his eyes roaming furtively about in the manner of cattle rustlers and chicken thieves.

Reluctantly, Arden K. lifted the dog's head and let it fall. Three times and a shadow appeared beneath the doorway.

"Is it?" asked the person on the other side.

"It is, and one more," Jeremy replied flatly, familiarly.

"Beware the sting of the bee for she knows all," said the hidden voice and Arden stepped backward as the door opened, expecting the ground to collapse beneath his feet, expecting to slide feetfirst down a secret shute once used for the storage of coal and dirty laundry, to land in some infernal sub-basement face to face with the diabolical and omnipotent Z.

In the deceptively cheery glow of yellow light streaming out onto the cobblestone surface of Patchin Place he saw a young girl, not much more than a child, holding a chimpanzee to her breast. The animal, dark and hairy, whimpering like an infant, was wearing a gold-painted dildo strapped to his body with a silver chain.

"Pongo suffers from satyriasis," the girl cordially

explained, extending her hand in welcome. "The doctor likes to keep him muzzled until he's needed. Won't you please come in, Mr. Hoffstetter. We've been expecting you," and she moved aside to let them pass.

What in the... and how in the world did she... but there was no time to ponder the half-said questions and Arden thought to himself, There's nothing like being an invited guest.

The door closed behind him and they moved into a narrow hallway cluttered with a random assortment of umbrellas, walking sticks, galoshes, and rubbers. (Of the latter, some were still packaged, and there were lubricated as well as dry varieties.) Arden tried to recall whether or not it had recently rained, but Jeremy asked impatiently, "Is she here? That's one of the reasons why we've come."

The child looked back at him, her face a perfect pendant for the most innocent of smiles. "The doctor has paraphrased wisely, from one not half as bright as he, saying that the demon of the twentieth century is no monster. He is merely a man depraved by vice."

"I know the dogma," Haberman snapped back.

"Then beware, brother. You think you are standing on high, yet beware of the descent and where you will descend," she replied with great mystery.

"Look, right now I only want to see the girl."

"She is being attended to. Everything comes with time."

So they tell me, Arden thought.

They followed behind her, reaching a much larger room with four leather couches, just like in Edward Albee's apartment. Candles flickered from corner niches, tables, sideboards, and credenzas. "I'll be back in a minute. Just make yourself comfortable," Haberman told him, taking the girl's hand and moving swiftly into the shadows.

Left alone in the withdrawing room without any of his own devices, Arden looked about, was at first intrigued and then mystified by the wallpaper which seemed to shine with a kind of phosphorescence all its own. He recognized the three great triptychs of Hieronymus Bosch: *The Hay Wagon, The Temptation of St. Anthony,* and *The Garden of Earthly Delights.* They had been blown up to cover the ornately paneled walls, and our friend and loved one made out, in the shifting light figures he recalled from Art Appreciation days, sexless coupled figurines and hybrid creatures performing acts of torture and depravity. Beneath one of the panels he found an inscription:

> *Quid sibi vult, Hieronyme Boschi,*
> *Ille oculus tuus attonitus? quid*
> *Pallor in ore? velut lemures si*
> *Spectra Erebi volitantia coram*
> *Aspiceres?*

But it was Latin to him, and his eyes moved on. He was so absorbed in studying what Mario Praz had called "the immodestly crouching white monster of Egoism" in the Hell panel of Bosch's most famous work, that he failed to hear footsteps approaching.

"It's probably too late!" Jeremy cried, rushing into the room and followed by a pack of three dogs, all pony-sized, with dripping jowls and other unappetizing evidences of acute excitement which closely, on a most superficial level, resembled that of rabid heat. For some stupid and no doubt outmoded Freudian reason the author is reluctant or just plain embarrassed to discuss canine *os penes.* I mean . . . would you be offended because I'm not, but more than likely this phallic fixation which has reappeared in other sections of the novel was brought on by a blow to the head received in childhood as a result of falling off a gelding. (Such obscure and mystical rhythms permeate the whole of this and future works, so there should be no immediate cause for undue alarm.)

"Where did they come from?" Arden asked, jumping up on the sofa and holding the animals at bay with the toe of his shoe.

"The doctor keeps them. Great Danes, Irish Wolf-hounds, St. Bernards, and some others. All the giant breeds. Actually, they're quite friendly. They just adore people, men especially. Don't you, sweetheart?" leaning over and nuzzling the nearest of his barking companions. "Relax, Arden. They're just turned on because you're a new face."

"Why does he keep them?" Hoffstetter asked when he had regained his composure and former position on the couch.

Jeremy sat down beside him and Arden saw flakes of white powder encrusted on his lips and nostrils. "Because...because he's free spirit. Because he lives without conscience. Because he owns a pet food factory. Because it pleases him, and his children."

Off somewhere else, Arden asked slyly, "Can I have some too? I could use it." His eyes still focused on the chalky residue around his friend's mouth and nose.

"Ah, *mon ami*, you see too much," running a finger over his lips and licking away some of the telltale evidence. "Coke is not good for growing boys."

"I'm all grown up. I even shave every day."

Haberman lifted his eyebrows. "Is that all?"

Arden decided to change the topic, asking, "Did you find the girl?"

"My key? No," Jeremy replied. "She must have already left with Z. The little bitch who opened the door, despite her marvelously retentive memory for things she's heard other people say, still has to be put in her place. The doctor doesn't like his children indulging in lies and fantasies. Anyway, we still have one more place to look.

But first I think it would be nice if you partook of some diversion. A little pleasure break to calm your nerves. You *are* nervous, aren't you?"

"I'm making a speedy recovery. This whole thing seems too ludicrous for words. The chimpanzee. This house. What's with all these Bosch pictures? And what does that Latin inscription mean over there?" pointing to the panel in question.

"That is Z's most favorite bit of verse. It's already been translated you know. I think it was by a Professor Casson or something like that."

"What does it mean?"

"Oh, roughly it goes like this," and he cleared his throat and took the stage to recite, "O, Hieronymus Bosch, what is the meaning of/that terrified eye of yours? What means/the pallor of your face? As if you were/seeing ghosts, specters of Hell shifting/before you?"

"Not very pleasant, is it."

"It sort of gets to you after awhile," Haberman said dreamily.

"You know quite a bit about Z. What's he like?"

"You're getting way ahead of yourself, Arden baby. Let's do one thing at a time. First the fun and games," and he rose to his feet.

"Are you sure we haven't been invited to a costume party? Somehow, I feel overdressed."

"That'll be the understatement of the year," Haberman grinned, displayed a most wicked chip in one of his front teeth which Arden had failed to notice before. "I will have to show you the other rooms, perhaps reveal a little more as best I can. Words seem positively paltry at a time like this. You know, I just can't have you leaving here without some word of explanation." He took Hoffstetter's hand and with securely intertwining fingers—a gesture Arden thought completely unnecessary—led him to a staircase at the other end of the room.

"A duplex. The man must have money," Arden said

gaily, prepared for a surprise party, champagne, bubbles, and The Lennon Sisters on the second floor.

But it's not my birthday, he thought as they mounted the stairs.

A thick cloying odor of incense greeted his nostrils. He had wanted to snort stronger stuff, but this non-too-unpleasant sensation would have to do for the present. He heard dogs barking and the mumbled muted voices of other people, but he was unsure of what direction they were coming from and quite unable to make out what was being said. At the top of the stairs, dark as is our American practice—and a very dangerous one at that—they stopped and Jeremy asked, "Which door?" motioning to two rooms on either side of the hallway.

"It doesn't matter, does it?"

"Not really," he said with a slight smile, pleased with Arden's answer. Still holding his hand, Haberman drew him to the doorway on the left, opened it swiftly and stepped inside.

The room seemed nothing more than a bed, a giant mattress upon which he made out the fornicating figures of a harlequin Great Dane, a Great Pyrenees, and a Bouvier des Flandres all somehow coupled, engaged, or serviced by young boys and girls, barely pubescent youths to judge by the hint of curl or fleecy tendril around their downy mounts.

"Don't say a word," Jeremy whispered, and Arden thought, I couldn't even if I wanted to.

Jeremy let go of Arden's hand and pulled him close, his hand encircling Hoffstetter's waist. "It gives the doctor pleasure, for he says that the highest degree of sanctity lies in following one's natural instincts."

"It depends on what you consider natural. How does he keep them here? What about their parents?" Arden asked, his feeling of immediate repulsion and dismay transforming itself first into amazement and then, almost against his better and more civilized will, into growing figurative and physical desire. He saw himself cavorting merrily in a most Edenic state of bliss and for the moment he fell prey to all his libertine dreams.

"Cocaine and heroin. The white slave trade. It's a wonder he hasn't been found out. Just imagine what his grocery bill must be like. But what do you think? Shall we join them?" spreading his legs apart and placing Arden's hand on the growing bulk in his pants.

"I really don't think it's my scene," Hoffstetter replied, losing his voice and jerking his hand away. "I'm sorry, Jeremy, I really am," and he turned to leave with the thought going through his mind that all his first impressions seemed terribly valid, horrifyingly real.

Haberman would not be put off so easily. "You'll never know until you try it," turning our hero around and forcing him up against the door. Then, without uttering a sound, he thrust his tongue into Arden's mouth. Hoffstetter struggled to release himself but in another moment he was pinned down by two of the lost children who giggled insanely, their eyes glazed and their bodies coated with perspiration and other biological fluids.

"Don't try to get free, Arden. You'll never be really free if you don't try what may be very good for you." Then, snapping his fingers to bring another pair of youngsters to his aid, Jeremy ordered them "Take off his clothes. I've been dying to see what she's been bragging about."

Arden strained his muscles to no avail. "Who?" he asked between suitably hostile and clenched teeth. "Bragging about what?"

"Questions, dearheart; you're always asking so many questions. Haven't you been warned about that by now?" said Jeremy Haberman, pinching Arden's cheek. Then, including all of the young people in the sweep of his voice, he revealed, "We shall initiate phase two and soon our ranks will be joined by yet another loyal brother of the sacred movement of the Free Spirit." He looked down at

Arden's livid face. "Don't struggle, baby. It won't hurt. You won't even feel a thing," running his fingers through Arden's hair. "It's only pleasure, for what else have we meager vulgar beings got in life but pleasure. I mean, just look what the war in Vietnam has done to our morality, so just relax and try to be a hedonist. It doesn't hurt, you know."

Hoffstetter's limbs went dead. He ceased to toss and thrash about and shut his eyes, knowing that nudity was not a commodity the public would approve of should he decide to take his opposition out onto the street. When all of his clothes were off they let him get to his feet, pointing to the bed where a Newfoundland dog waited with a matched set of Italianate youths the likes of which Caravaggio would have given his eyeteeth to paint.

"You win," he told Haberman, grim and outwardly resigned, but as soon as they let go of him he bolted for the door, slamming it closed behind him as the dogs began their barking and the children squealed with rage. Without hesitating, his vulnerability etched on the surface of his birthday suit, he ran to the other side of the dimly illumined corridor and pushed open the door to the second room.

"Belinda!" he shouted, seeing his neighbor lying naked in a supine position upon an oriental rug.

"Well, it's about time," she said distastefully fingering her perfect, merkin-like mons; her motions detached like a page from a book of quick and easy thrills. "I thought you might have gotten caught in a subway jam." At that moment a figure emerged out of the pervading darkness, wreathed in shadows at the other end of the room. It moved forward and Arden recognized one of Bernie Guysman's superstars.

"The Ainu!" he shouted incredulously, referring to the most infamous member of that primitive and hirsute Japanese race, who should have been in Karafuto or

Hokkaido, not New York. "What's going on here?"

"We're having a little party. An unbirthday party," replied Belinda.

The Ainu carried a live chicken, white and squawking, in both of his hands, his body richly greased, anointed, and fully aroused. He walked slowly as if carefully rehearsed, his manhood bouncing up and down like a tree caught in a storm.

"You'd think it was Yom Kippur," Belinda laughed, arching her back and honey pot invitingly. "Do your stuff, Sol. Do it for your favorite queen bee," she told the actor.

The chicken stretched its neck, tried to free its wings which the Ainu held in place. Feathers rustled and flew, and the bird cackled as if the henhouse had just been invaded by every fox in the state. But ever so carefully, ever so methodically, the oriental pulled the bird down over his remarkably trenchant staff.

"My God, I'm getting sick," dry-mouthed Arden choked out a whisper. "I think I'm going to throw up," but at that nauseous and dizzy instant, as the shock of his bewilderment flew out of his throat and into the air, he felt his head being crushed in, pounded from within and without and everything went spinning off into impenetrable blackness as he crumpled to the floor.

"Life is sometimes as improbable as fiction," Belinda had said to him one day not too long ago. "But I should think that one would get far greater satisfaction living it than writing about it."

"Why can't one do both?" Arden replied, stroking the cat who lay nestled, sleeping in his lap.

"I suppose you can. You can try, I mean. But don't you find yourself fragmenting? Don't you sort of separate and become both observer and participant?"

"Yes and no."

"That's what I love about you, Hoffstetter. Always

there to give the definitively incisive statement," she said sarcastically. "The question that comes to mind however, right at this instant, is whether or not a person can go on indefinitely playing at such calculated schizophrenia."

They were sitting together at the kitchen table, the remains of an afternoon tea scattered around them. She put a finger to her mouth, moistened it with her tongue and began to pick up some of the crumbs: English muffins, raisin bread, Danish butter cookies. "Well," she persisted. "Can you?"

"Why intellectualize on the creative process. Only people who aren't terribly creative themselves have to search out answers to reveal the inner workings of an artist's mind. I do. I exist. I observe. I write. I am me. All these things. I don't know, or at least not on a conscious level, why I do what I do, why I have to write, why I feel this incredible urge. I just react, usually without much forethought. I'm a creature of impulse, if you must know the truth."

"Splendid," she laughed, clapping her hands. "Sounds marvelous, but what happens when you're discovered."

"How so?"

"What happens when you're found out, when someone suddenly realizes that you aren't what you say you are, that it really isn't Arden K. Hoffstetter sitting before them, but two people. Arden the writer who watches from the other side of the room, telling Arden the living, the person, what to say and how to react to every situation."

"But it isn't that way at all," he protested.

"But you just told me that it was. That you were two people working at odds with each other."

"I never said anything of the sort," he replied, his voice rising above the level of politeness. "All I said was that I react without making plans. Elaborate beforehand preparations. My observations come back to me when I sit down in front of my typewriter."

"Tell me," she interrupted. "When you're in bed with

someone, do you see yourself then as two different Ardens? One the physical and the immediate, the other the distant and pensive analyzer."

At this he laughed and his amusement woke the cat who stretched on his lap and jumped on top of the table, working its tongue into the half-filled creamer. "When I'm screwing I cease to watch myself performing. The few times I used to intellectualize on balling, I found myself going limp, so now I just do and enjoy. How's that for total masculine honesty?"

She smiled absently, looking beyond him to something on the wall which appeared to have claimed her attention, so that he heard her saying, "Then there's hope for the world and the reading public," not as if Belinda was there, but just a shadow like a discarded snakeskin inhabiting her body, while her thoughts and emotions floated off in search of distant pleasures and new experiences.

That night, he did not feel at peace with the world, or even the reading public, for that matter.

"Pauline and Austin are caught in a net under the sea," begins a rather mediocre second novel we read recently, purchased for a dollar at a publisher's overstock sale. For the net under the sea is composed of the stuff of dreams—fleeting and evanescent are the usual adjectives applied—and we proceed headlong through a series of highly pretentious metaphysical images before we confront the character awake and functioning, moving sluggishly amidst the appurtenances of soap and water, toothpaste and black coffee. Indeed, for the past few years it has been considered quite *à la mode* to either inject French idioms or dream sequences into the content of serious fiction. Not to be outdone and after careful consideration of the facts, we have decided to indulge in a bit of surrealistic reverie, if only to make our novelistic efforts that much more palatable in the eyes of critical judgment and opinion.

ARDEN'S DREAM: Arden dreamed he was on a train, which is supposed to suggest vague psychosexual connotations, similar to horseback riding.

Everyone was standing, holding on to poles or straps, thin as a number two pencil, and he squeaked in a tiny tremolo, "Help! My pencil isn't sharpened and someone has stolen my eraser so now I can't even begin to correct my mistakes!" which is, in case you weren't aware, a typical remark often heard on the subway.

A man held up a Scottie puppy for Arden's inspection "Is its belly too distended?" he asked, greatly terrierized. "I knew I shouldn't have purchased a bargain pup."

Then the subway train stopped, but the doors remained stuck and all the pencils cried and melted so that Arden shouted in a marvelous subterranean vibrato, "How can I write without my pencil? My typewriter is missing a ribbon. Someone with evil in their eye has stolen my ribbon!"

A detective with a silver badge engraved "DICK" came out of nowhere into somewhere holding a copy of the Walker Report and questioned him with a trace of profuse professionalism. "I think it was the green parachutist who threw it away in free fall. Or was it free-for-all?"

"No, she left to visit her cousin Zooey who had to tell her about a dog he went out with. I know, because I saw her get on the train. If only she would have taken a ride with me, I'm sure everything would have been all right," Arden replied, suddenly losing his voice and beginning to shrink with amazing science-fictional agility.

"Don't step on the humble author," the detective told the crowd of melted pencils. "Even though everyone else does, it's still an infraction of the Health Code that'll land you nine to five in the city morgue, plus time off for good behavior."

The puddle that was Arden the Voiceless, Arden the shrunken pool of human liquid, slid across the sloping subway floor all the while keeping himself aloof from the other puddles, then higgledy-piggledy down a flight of rickety steps and out into the sunlight where he congealed and stood erect, thrust out his chest and squinted like a pro-simian at the pale savannah. "Something has gone amiss with the miss," he mused with an ejaculatory sigh. "Am I stoned or have I been stoned, that is the question?"

"Neither," said a voice, invisible in the meadow of graphite grass and he moved his head from side to side, dizzy and still nauseous. He explored the world with his fingertips, felt a surface which was both cold and smooth and he opened his eyes.

ARDEN'S DREAM (IS NOW OVER). THE END OF IT: Indeed, everyone was waiting, breathless and triumphant, impatient as well, for the outcome of Arden K.'s coming-out.

They would not wait for too much longer as he now awakes in a bathtub without any clothes on.

Before he could be made aware of anything else, he touched his body tentatively, and from an inner and totally unfamiliar uncomfortable sensation he realized with horror that he had been violated beyond the bounds of human decency. "Shades of Uranus!" he cried aloud, employing the appropriate cryptocosmic allusion. "I've been sodomized!"

"Great Caesar's ghost, darling. Have some slivovitz; it'll refresh you," said Belinda, acting like a cold-hearted Eurasian bitch. She got up from the bathroom floor of black and white checkered tiles and handed him a plum-colored brandy glass. "You've been a long time coming to. Everyone has fallen asleep."

Arden worked himself into a sitting position inside the tub. "My head," he groaned, exploring the surface of his scalp with an investigatory finger. "What happened? I must have blacked out or something."

"I'm afraid you were hit on the head by a blunt but

non-lethal weapon," she replied, quite calm and collected as is a lady of leisure. "Frankly, I'd hoped you would have a stronger stomach. You let me down, Arden. You know that, don't you."

"I don't know anything. Why am I in a bathtub? Why was I taken advantage of? It's like necrophilia. Here I was unconscious throughout the whole dirty brown business. It's just disgusting. And I hurt," he concluded with a whimper that would have drawn tears from even the most stouthearted of men.

"Well, you don't think you would have submitted willingly, do you? The pain is psychological, because it was quite carefully executed, I assure you and it was only part of the ritual. Everyone has to go through the ritual one way or another."

He replied, "I would have preferred another, thank you."

She looked at him quite earnestly. "Look, I went through it too. Same as you."

"I draw no comfort from that, especially when it's me who's still in pain," he answered, when he suddenly took a look at the palm of his right hand. "What is this supposed to mean?" he asked angrily, sticking his hand in her face. Upon the surface of his skin were the tiny tattooed letters: FSM.

"The Free Speech Movement," Belinda explained without batting an eye. "We try to coordinate our activities."

"I'm sure it means something quite different. I'm not that much of a fool." Shakily he got to his feet. "If I ever get hold of that sonuvabitch Haberman, he'll have plenty to answer for."

"You will."

"When?" he demanded.

"Soon. We're supposed to meet him down on Broome Street."

"And what time is it now, darling? You forget: I haven't slept."

"Nor have I," but she obliged him by glancing at her watch. "Nearly three in the morning. Don't worry, Arden. It'll all be over in a couple of hours. I promise you."

"What'll be over?" and finding his clothes piled neatly on top of the toilet, he began to get dressed.

"This whole thing."

"Belinda, maybe I'm asking too much, but at this moment, aside from not feeling anything like my old self, would you kindly do me the honor of a little explanation. Just a word or two, if you don't mind."

"Why can't you just partake of things, instead of always sitting back and asking questions? We're trying to cure you of that."

"First of all, I didn't sit back, and second of all, who is *we*?"

"The FSM. It's bound to make you a better person in the long run. Even Mona thinks so."

"Oh, so now Mona rears her ugly head," he said bitterly. "How did she get involved, may I ask?"

"She introduced you to Jeremy, didn't she?"

"Am I supposed to be flattered? First Haberman, then you, then the Ainu. Everyone's getting into the act. Are you going to sit there and say that they're all doing it for Arden K. Hoffstetter? I'm not nearly as naive as everyone seems to think."

"Think whatever you like. In the long run you'll see how much a better person you will have become."

"In the long run, in the long run," he bitched. "In the long run I may very well have a nervous breakdown. I'm happy the way I am," he told her, putting the finishing touches on his costume. "I like myself. I like what I stand for. I like where my head is at. I don't want to change."

"Sometimes we have to do what we don't want to do,

or even what we don't like to do. We can't always have our way," she replied curtly.

"Well, at least I'm getting good material." He put his hand to the door. "Promise me that when I step outside I won't be attacked by anyone."

"Don't worry. I told you that they all went to Broome Street."

"What's on Broome Street?"

"You'll see. Ready to go?" she asked with a smile, gathering her things together.

Arden looked at her suspiciously. "The dogs, too?"

"No, silly. They're all bedded down. Sleeping peacefully. They certainly were put through their paces tonight, so it's no wonder they're all exhausted."

He sneered at her. "I'm glad for them. I'm glad for you. I'm glad for Jeremy, for the whole world, for the FSM, but when I see him I'm going to..."

"Going to do nothing. Listen baby, the Homintern has nothing whatsoever to do with us. Jeremy is as straight as you or me, probably even more so. Do you really think he enjoyed playing the role? Let me assure you that he didn't, but he did it for you. For you, Arden. To open your eyes. Only a man can sponsor another man. That's how the rules work."

"And who thought up these rules?"

"Before you or I were ever born. Thought up just to let us see that differences exist between people which must be conquered if we're ever going to live in a saner world. Be a little more perceptive, sweetheart. It's all I ask."

"Anal perversion leads to brotherhood, is that what you're saying? Follow me through the back door and we'll end up being more effective than the U.N. What a lot of horseshit!"

"I can see already that it will take far longer than this evening to make a man out of you."

"Anything else?" he asked her. "I thought I've heard all there is to tell."

"Not yet, but almost." Then she followed him into the corridor, down the stairs, through the front rooms and out into the stark quiet of an empty street.

Chapter 7¹/₂

"A Further Misadventure of Das Wunderkind" is now published for the first time. Arden K. Hoffstetter wrote it nearly twenty years ago, late in the 1980's, at a time when his journal reveals his growing self-doubts and recurring dreams of premature death. It is now thought to be the beginning of a new novel, one which would have incorporated those elements of the Free Spirit movement which Hoffstetter so admired. Although his official biography makes no mention of the work, nor does Professor Heidener Oberfest in his definitive bibliography, it is assumed that Hoffstetter was working on this fragment just before his tragic and untimely death. It was not until two years ago that the manuscript was discovered by Jeremy Haberman, during a routine annual inspection and cataloguing of items in the Hoffstetter Archives. Why it remained hidden and unnoticed all this time is still cause for speculation.

Though the work was originally typewritten, as opposed to the author's own erratic and distinctive calligraphy, verification of authenticity was able to be made with the use of the very latest radioisotopic techniques. Now, thanks to the Estate of Arden K. Hoffstetter which has authorized its publication, the general public can share what we consider to be a singularly unique, instructive, and rewarding literary experience.

Hoffstetter wrote or transcribed this chapter section

without changes, typewritten on both sides of eight shirt cardboards of the kind once readily obtained at Chinese hand laundries. The lower righthand corner of each stiff paper sheet bears the following hand-stamped notation: "We do all high-class work and good service. Not responsible for fire, burglary, colors that fade, goods left over 30 days or loss of ticket. Unless itemized list is sent with goods, our count must be accepted." (The original manuscript may be examined with proper authorization on every second Tuesday of each month. Appointments must be made in advance through the office of the Director of Cultural History, Museum of Literary Arts & Sciences, Kennedy, D.C.) No evidences of rough drafts are now extant, but it is safe to conclude that such in-progress versions once existed. It is known that the author frequently destroyed all drafts and variants but his final one, for fear that his work habits would be too carefully scrutinized without regard for the nuances of his stylistic technique.

What sets the work above the level of merely being a fascinating curio is that it heralds what appears to be a marked departure from Hoffstetter's previous style as embodied in *Flush, Spit, Coprolight,* and other works; encompassing dispassionate egoistic elements the author apparently and successfully suppressed for most of his adult life. What is now left open in its wake is our ability to perceive a totally new side of Hoffstetter's world, a world whose emotions and perceptions have been continually arresting the imaginations of scholars for nearly a quarter of a century.

D.B.Z.

Nova Rangoon, 25 October A.I.D.

A FURTHER MISADVENTURE OF DAS WUNDERKIND

I was born under the mushroom cloud, a child of my

time always aware of the Death Angel *Amanita phalloides*. But I survived this and other contemporary ordeals and grew up to be loved from afar.

Actually, when you come right down to it, it would be easy to say that I am loved by all, the masses in particular. Of course, there are always those others that could argue the other way—that I'm the belover, not the beloved. Far be it from me to dwell upon the mere semantics of that side issue. But my landlady thinks I'm terribly well-put-together, cute, textured, and high-blown; she never has explained the last. Yet sometimes, like after I've downed three-in-a-row cups of her fabulous brew, my mouth making crumbs out of the last blueberry muffin, she'll scratch herself demurely and remark, sort of casual and off-the-cuff, "You know dear, you're awfully terribly high-blown." She keeps asking me down for coffee and Lost Generation muffins, so I suppose the term is vaguely complimentary. I do hope so.

And then there's this girl, if I dare call her that, who lives down the hall, always muttering, *"C'est domage, mon petit,"* as she hurries down the stairs to catch the 8:05 monorail. Which, in a crackerjack nutshell, goes to prove that I am everybody's *mon petit* and that's why I look with confidence at the prospect of tomorrow, knowing that the masses find me exhilarating.

For nigh onto twenty some-odd years or so, give or take a few millennia, they've called me Magnificent. Manley Magnificent to be more exact. It was, from my earliest mother taught ego-recollections on the subject, "Manley Magnificent, you're just too much," and "Manley, you're God's fair-haired gift to everyone at large." I could have made a career out of it, selling options on my good looks to ad agencies and Hollywood talent scouts. Could have made a mint by now posing with and for all the name brands, drinking and smoking according to the dictates of the market. Can't you just see, my name in flickers of orange neon, running along the Allied Chem

Tower: MANLEY MAGNIFICENT DRINKS...AND M.M. WEARS...ALL THE TIME. I sleep in the nude, between two off-white sheets and a khaki army blanket that has seen better days distant years ago at mountain retreats.

Now I wouldn't be dragging you into this if I didn't feel that you loved me, because the story is kind of personal (in a high-blown sort of way) and well, just that. You know how it is, so please bear with all the scruffy spiffy details. The whole thing was so long in coming out of my glib void I call my brain that now I'm almost afraid to reveal the whole sordid mess. Not *that* sordid, but perhaps classifiable as possibly obscene. I'll leave that up to all your loving doting discretions.

"All beginnings are difficult," says a holy book of a dying culture, and I tend to agree. But I might as well start somewhere. Let us then face our hero, yours truly, squarely and forwardly about two years ago. It was on one of those blissful September evenings when the stars are promenading across the deepest of gentian skies, and girls with stylish Sassoon bobs hold down their macro skirts as they mince up along old Fifth Avenue. The clubs, C-parlors, and infamous nights spots were doing a swift business, judging by the number of chauffeured cars lined up in front of every fashionably hidden and smart hotel in this part of town. There were all sorts queuing up by the entrances of local cinemas. It looked like everyone had decided that tomorrow just might be the big mushroom day, and they weren't taking any chances about missing a final evening of fun and frolic.

Newspaper gusts of recirculated city air were thrown up all around me, and I remember hunching my shoulders and playing a resurrected Lemmy Caution, with the trench buckled tight and the painted grimace of a sad clown full grown adorning my face. I got to the St. Regis, cast an all-knowing inquiring glance at the glass-eyed doorman, and walked up the red-carpeted steps, through the revolving kiosk doors and into the lobby. Now you must remember that I was the golden-haired youth of all time, way back to nearly pre-war then. But my looks have reached that wonderful point of encumbrance that people approach me to ask with brazen indifference to my feelings, "Haven't I read about you?" or "Aren't you so-and-so's latest character in that new sex scorcher, what's-its-name?" Which means to imply that this youth's beauty is so overpowering that it is apt to assume a quality of fictional estrangement from the more mundane practices and realities of everyday existence. But really, only that everybody is trying to make me, in the hardest way possible, and the terrible tragic truth is that it's so easy. But few have tried; they all seem to think it's impossible to come within goosing distance of the boy wonder. Even the landlady, playing the unrequited lover, always hands me my morning coffee with an extended hand and well-manicured fingernails, always afraid to beckon me closer, to even touch.

So, at the moment, I was without the comfort of warm flesh on this chilly autumnal eve. Reason among the synaptic connections had it that if I watched the others at play, sooner or later I would become one with them, merging and touching in a dynamic surge of protoplasm. At long last, to become . . . but, to continue.

I was standing in a state of obvious contemplation, rooted like a rare flower in the middle of the lobby when a man with orange-tinted glasses, silvery hair, and a cutaway coat came up from behind and tapped me on the shoulder.

"This way," he motioned. "I can't talk now. Too many people."

"Pardon?"

"This way, young man," and he turned into the dining room, walking so that you could barely see the heels of his patent leather pumps. I followed, squeezing around tables and embarrassing waiters poised with loaded trays, until I got to the bar and found a champagne split and a lit cigarette waiting for me.

"What do you mean, kind sir, by removing me from a position where I could feel that dynamic surge?" I demanded, swallowing the drink in a single silenced gulp. The cigarette, Orient Express 999, had a crimson mark where my lips were destined to be.

"Quiet! Please," he implored. "She gave that to me to deliver personally," pointing to the cigarette. "Said you would understand."

"But of course," I replied. "Orient Express. Best grass in the world. But who is She?"

He stared at me for a few seconds, perhaps afraid I was not the youth he sought. Then, shocked at my lack of recognition, he uttered between pinched lips, "Surely you jest, Magnificent."

I refused to be cowered by his knowledge of my name. "I am afraid I do not, sir."

He shrugged. "You'll know her when you meet. In fact, you've met before. But this must all be done with the utmost of discretion. I'd have it no other way."

"Nor would I," and I motioned the bartender over for another round. "Will you join me?" I asked, adding in a voice deeply resonant and thrill-evoking, "Frangere."

His heels visibly clicked as I uttered his name. "How do you know who I am? She promised it would all be done with discretion. Second-person references only."

"Your coat," I explained, "is conveniently embroidered."

"Those damned fool Hong Kong tailors," he muttered. The orange tint of his lenses seemed to cover his entire face.

The moment the last of the second round had passed between my unkissed lips he was dragging me by the belt of the trench, très discreetly, back into the lobby, down the steps to the lower level, past the barber shop, the phone booths, the bootblack's stand. "Are you a homosexual?" I inquired politely, after he had paused in the center of the men's restroom, balancing himself on the heels of his shoes. The soles were silvery metal, and I was surprised that I hadn't heard their staccato clicking before.

He caught my stare. "Oh, no."

The bare tile floor captured my reflection, made it woozy and unclear, and the sparkle of the mirrors above the wash-basins made it difficult for me to see my face. Not that I'm a mirror boy, never was, doubt if I shall ever become one. Vanity is unnecessary when the rest of humanity mirrors my looks in their every glance.

Through here. Follow carefully." He opened the door to one of the stalls. "Don't soil your trousers." I maintained a good six feet to the rear.

"I fail to understand what this is leading up to, mister," I began in a more hostile tone. "I usually don't care for public sex, and homosex in the men's john is just, shall I say, a little bit too passé."

At that moment the rear wall, behind the toilet, had disappeared, and with a voice that was not his own he called back, "Nonsense. That isn't my style. Not even during the years I prepped. Are you coming?"

"I suppose," and I found myself squeezing behind the porcelain to enter a narrow corridor. No sooner had my feet grazed the threshold when the concealing panel closed against my back. On either side deep red brick, slightly moist; up ahead Frangere, and beyond him a hint of greater illumination.

"What is this?" I whispered.

"Nothing much. A secret corridor I had installed for her several years ago, right after her coming-out. Rather convenient, don't you think?"

"If you like the St. Regis," I replied with a snort, saying in the same breath, "But where are you taking me?"

Against the dripping brick a thousand little whispering Herculean devils echoed back, catching and tossing my voice along the walls.

"Must you?" he asked, raising his hands to cup his ears. "It's bad enough when they flush."

In the dimness of the passageway I became positive that there were no eyes behind his orange lenses. And just as this horrifying feeling of the macabre was settling like a death sheet, a hideous shroud which brought to the neck of the trench the wetness of acute anxiety, I perceived a gradual increase in the light's intensity. Calming down, my ears caught the sound of people not far away. "Will she be thrilled to see me?" I asked.

He turned his head back, slowing down to a shuffle. "Oh very. She'll be very pleased, yes very. You see," he confided with unfounded familiarity, "she's been looking forward to this little encounter for the longest time now."

"You don't say? How wonderful!"

"For the longest," he continued, not letting my sarcasm get in his way. "And now that you've finally made it . . . What can I say?"

"Tell me how wonderful I am."

Strains of familiar movie music, snatches of reminiscent words, flowed along the walls like a ribbon's-length of the finest grosgrain. At last Frangere reached a point of maximum illumination, and opening what appeared to be a thick door of rose-colored glass, we entered a brilliantly lit vestibule, lined on either side by evening capes, furs of every style and species, and other such paraphernalia.

"At last," he declared with a sigh of relief, and throwing off his tailed coat, but giving me no time to remove the trench, he poised a loaded finger before my eyes and silently I acquiesced, following him down the foyer where he opened another door.

Immediately the pieces of sound were glued together. Here were voices of Protestant aspiration, throat sounds juggling between today and tomorrow, moving lips extolling the power of prestige, ancestral glory, the hunt. He let me listen for a moment, and as if content with the initial effect, I was hustled back to the entrance room. The door closed once again, the words faded into mute reminders, but my eyes had watched, had seen their eyes flip toward me as mouths moved into smiles, lips parted slightly but significantly—moistened with pink dabs of tongue, necks turning fractions of inches in intense study. A successful debut. An easily won victory.

My hands had thrust themselves deep into the trench pockets and, recalling Caution's better days, I rocked back and forth with the linger of a sensual grimace so very well practiced upon my magnificent-to-behold visage.

"Frangere, you darling gofor. How ever did you manage it?"

Without turning my head, I answered for my chaperon. "And so discreetly, not a single unjustified squawk," snickering slightly. "But haven't we met before? The Prado perhaps, or the films at Marienbad?" A poor antiquated jest, but deliberately used to deploy my confidence in the hope of upsetting hers.

"Still the same, Magnificent. How I adore your boyish charm, your fragile witticisms. You haven't lost any of it in all these years." From the corner of my eye I watched She move up behind me, watched two veiled arms slide over my shoulders and down my trench, unbuckling the last remnants of my ace expatriate's greatest days. I spun around with deliberate force, my eyes rooted into hers, my head cocked slightly to emphasize my good side. (Though both are equally stunning, I still have my preferences.)

"No one ever touches. If you'll be so kind as to show me to the door, there are Others waiting." In dark corners, hidden crevices, shadowed alleys of the twilight hours, and the zones of fear and soundless screams of a latter-day Tondalus; there they are waiting, waiting for my next move, my next mistake. I had never seen her face, not that

I forget faces—I never do—but hers was totally new, fresh in the history of genetic permutations. Exquisitely colored skin, shades of mother-of-pearl and the pink sands of tropical islands; forgetting, unforgiving eyes.

"The 'Others' are all here. No one of importance or consequence is out there. You will learn that in time. Here, let me take your coat; you must be dreadfully overheated."

"And inconvenienced." Yet strangely enough, the power behind her words made my arms slip out of the sleeves.

"You may wait for me inside," she indicated the door that had recently opened and closed for my presence. With a drink in my hand, I went off to a corner to watch the proceedings.

In a large room, half as long as it was wide, grapelike clusters of men and women were engaged in conversation, sipping steam cocktails and smoking chocolate paper joints with silver roach holders. Overhead, enormous Tiffany lamps illuminated the interior. The pocked and stippled wall surfaces were almost entirely covered by an array of oversized paintings. For the moment I was reminded of my great-aunt Zina's house, where her murky parlor was wrapped in neo-Raphaelite creations, little silver icon lamps perched above each work of art. The selections here were all in identical frames, bereft of spotlighting, deep ebony wood with calligraphic gold trim—antique gold, the kind you can buy in little spray cans. I turned back to see if She had returned when something clicked.

Obviously *mes chères*, the time was nil for the epiphany. But the realization—certainly!—that was what it was! The remembrance of the Prado came back to me like a nightmare call: the reproductions were all of works by Bosch. The old master, Hieronymus B., also van Aken. And Frangere: where had I heard of him before? Along my left was a giant hell scene, resplendent with sulfur fires, wondrous musical instruments of torture, monsters constructed from the debris of a diseased imagination. On the right, closest to me, neuterized doll-people supped from berries the size of basketballs, swam with elephantine birds in glass pools, made love beneath fishbowls of the purest transparency. I was all too sure: at last I had found them. This was where I had to be, where I was destined to be. The rumors were often scorned. I had refused to believe the secret tales, but now, now it was all going to become real and apparent. I remembered the old woman on the square, the quaint flower vendor, and stepping back into daylight. After peering at the originals along the gloomy Spanish walls she had uttered those now infamous words: *"Cave, cave frater, quia tu credis stare in alto, sed caveas de descensu et quomodo descendes."* I, creature of laughter, English, and derision, innocent of the ordeals of Fra Giovannuccio da Bevagna, bought a penny bunch of nosegays and kept walking. Now it was crystalline, held immovable and totally inevitable. Inevitable that I should be standing with this mimosa, steam spiked, all eye corners glued to my every move, as if waiting for the master himself to appear. In the guise of the beloved symbol of universal sexuality . . . who but the Boy Wonder!

"Are you introverted? Surely I never would have thought that."

"I never come on very strong," I told her. "It's all part of my charm."

"Frangere tells me that you gave him quite a difficult time back there. You almost had me fooled."

"Me too," and I swallowed what remained in the glass.

"And now, how totally boring it must be for you." She twisted the strand of black pearls that hung, as if suspended, from her alabaster throat, her eyes never leaving mine. "I do hope you'll put up with all the coming

207

introductions. I know it was horribly indecent of me not to forewarn you, but that is how things are I'm afraid, and now that you're here..."

"Does it matter? No excuses, please," I replied. "I thank Frangere for giving me the pleasure of not introducing you. I am Magnificent. Feel free to call me that, or Manley if you prefer the more austere." I was being so diplomatic, leaving all openings.

She was visibly perplexed, but caught her poise on a fleeting kiss to my lips and went on to say, "Yes, I know. No need to recall past unpleasantries. For now you may wish to call me Lois. It is simple enough. They," motioning to her mass of guests, "refer to me as that, or more often as She. Terribly H. Rider Haggard, but it amuses me. But take your pick; I leave the choice entirely to your own good taste." At long last her eyes blinked, revealing gold-tinted lids. The fragrance of melony musk floated lazily in the air, unhampered by things which were to follow. "And now," taking my arm, "it is time we made you a man." We moved forward into this new calf's maw of humanity.

Chapter 8

CHEAP THRILLS are a dime a dozen.

Our Arden, our sweetheart, just wanted to sleep. Just wanted to have a glass of milk and a brace of chocolate chip cookies. Just wanted to brush his teeth and take off his shoes, maybe even shower. Simple things. Not that he didn't like swinging. But swinging was fine on Friday and Saturday nights, conventional nonbusiness nights. It just wasn't what he wanted; he just wasn't ready to handle weekday bouts of nocturnal depravity. It wasn't his bag.

Our Arden, our plumface, born under the mushroom cloud of days filled with false security, was now nearing the end of this twisting trail, this twisted tale. The forest was thinning and in the distance he could make out the purple riders, shadow figures in a land of unpleasant dreams. He thought to himself, Everything is finally falling into place.

But really, he didn't understand what it all meant, even though it sounded nice. Different. Perhaps even a trifle bizarre. Intriguing if nothing else.

"I'm resigned," he announced, breaking his self-imposed silence. Ever since leaving the house on Patchin Place he had not said a word. He had accepted the presence of a large black limousine, shiny and sleek in the streetlamp glow, without comment, following Belinda into the back seat and even locking the door behind him. He had inhaled the rich fragrance of hand-tooled leather, his nostrils tasting and savoring future dividends of the good life. But he had said nothing, nary a sound. He had planned it this way.

"I'm resigned," he said again when he failed to elicit a response, tearing apart the fragile tissue of silence and mortal dread with three clumsy syllables.

"To what?" the girl asked.

"To failure. To change. I'm learning, even now, to accept the inevitable. I'll even go through with it."

"And be a good sport? And look like an ass-kisser?"

"I'm not answering any more questions," he replied without emotion. "First you tell me one thing and you criticize my life style, and then you say something else, something entirely different. I don't ask questions, but I sure as hell won't answer any."

"You're very strange," she mused as the long and anonymous car wove through the empty downtown streets, past rows of black brownstones and bargain boutiques.

"Belinda," he began again with great seriousness. "Am I or am I not being big about this? What more do you expect from me?"

"Lots."

"What? I've just about given away my soul, my identity. I'm reacting without any of the necessary answers, without a single grain of understanding. Do you think I know what's going on? Do you *really* think that?"

"But it doesn't matter. Watch and accept. If you've given away your soul, you still have your spirit. You must part with that as well, and give in to things that don't come sifting down from the inside of your head."

It was not the answer he had hoped for, and bitterly he replied, "*Deus videt*, just remember that."

"What?"

"God sees. God sees, so beware when you start to tamper with a person's head."

"God sees only love, Arden. Nothing else. He is blind to iniquities, blind to faith. But he sees love because he is love."

"Sister Belinda, champion of the rights of the oppressed. Hah!"

"Champion of the free spirit. . . ."

"Just fuck off, okay," he interrupted angrily, rage mounting steeply behind his words. "I've had it, kid. Just about all I can take. Isn't it time you called off your little pack of playmates?"

"And spoil the game, especially when it isn't even over?" she said with a smile, unctuous to the extreme. Then, rapping to the unseen driver, "The corner'll be fine."

The car reacted like a cliché and slid noiselessly to a halt.

"Are you coming?" she asked.

"I don't have any other choice, do I?"

"No. It's either all or nothing. I'd take the former."

Reluctantly, sorry to give up this small amount of luxury, he followed her out of the car as dampness and early morning mist pressed in about them. The limousine sped around a corner and was gone and they were now alone at what could be the beginning or the end of just about anything he had ever dreamed of.

Roundups are the worst.

Pat finales with lavish production numbers are no better.

Yet no one likes loose ends. They much prefer to see life labeled, boxed and canned, put into shiny glass jars, preserved on a shelf. Leave a reader with unanswered questions, leave him puzzled, and he'll hate you for the rest of his life. That's how things are. Therefore, we are sorry if at the end—which is soon enough to come—there will be some of you who will turn away with disappointment. This is not meant to be an apology, mind you, for writers are above such things, even above explanations. It is just another of our *deus ex machina* interruptions guaranteed to startle the unwary. Actually, we had intended (hopefully) to entertain and enlighten you, never realizing in our zealous good faith and striving toward perfection that you might want to live vicariously, that you just might want to wrap us all up and toss us into the litter basket of your unconscious. Again, we are sorry, for life is a compilation of loose ends and fragile beginnings, of people who disappear in and out of our days, never to return. Of extraordinary experiences that lose the sharp edge of distinction as days pass into long-forgotten memories and we turn toward the future, rather than the past.

For Arden, however, time would not ease the burdens that he was soon to bear. Responsible only to his own happiness, that well-balanced fulcrum of internal stability, he would draw away from this night and morning with mixed feelings, knowing—if nothing else— that selfishness and insularity made people stale and mediocre, never giving. Never aware of the possibilities of unexpected intrusions into the course of random events, never alive to the green fuse of creativity which ignites the spirit and inflames the heart.

"Name?"

"I have no name," he answered, curt and brief, defiant and feeling like a freedom fighter, a white-hatted good guy torn from the pages of a Grade B western.

"What do you mean, you have no name?" Belinda interjected with a hiss. "Tell him your name instead of making life difficult for everyone."

"Faceless. Mindless. Failure," he went on, glum and withdrawn into a kind of passive sphere of glass, a crystal egg which proved but a meager shelter from the world outside. Looking about him as he stood rigid and unmoving, he caught no hint, captured no clue. There was nothing worthy of examination in this small square room of paint-peeled walls and floor of scratched and blackened linoleum.

"Name?"

"Arden Hoffstetter."

"Name?"

"Arden K. Hoffstetter."

"Name?"

"I have no name."

"Name?"

"We can go on all night, you know...."

"Name?"

"Arden Kendrick Hoffstetter."

"Birthplace?"

"This big wide wonderful land."

"Birthplace?"

"Wisconsin."

"Religion?"

"Atheist."

"Religion?"

"None at the moment. May I make a point of personal preference?" he asked, remembering the rules from his days of being a committee member.

"No. Age?"

"Thirty years."

"Occupation?"

"I wouldn't hazard a guess."

"Occupation?"

"Reader of unsolicited manuscripts on a free-lance basis."

"Thank you," the voice behind the screen replied, and pages turned, rustle of cloth and paper, and there were long moments of unrelieved silence during which Arden K. shifted from one foot to another, painfully pained, painfully unamused.

"Do you have anything else to say, Arden Kendrick Hoffstetter, before passing through?"

"I have suffered long and hard," he said with all the restraint his voice could muster. "I have been beset by treachery at every step. I have been raped against my will."

"That, of course, is implied in the definition. But is that all?"

Arden replied, "For now."

"I too have been raped, though not in the exact manner which you have undergone. I too have been trodden upon, have seen my friends and loved ones turn on me, so that now I have become but a paragraph, perhaps only a sentence in this book, a string of words in an uncompleted novel. I am a line of 12 point Video Times Roman type set by electronic composition on an IBM 360 Computer and an RCA Videocomp. So I suffer, needlessly perhaps, but suffer nevertheless. For I too have been set at tasks against my will. Yet I have learned, Arden Hoffstetter. I have learned just as you must. You may pass," and from behind the screen the sound of table rapping issued forth. Three knocks and Arden closed his eyes, trying to recall the past and persuade himself that he would soon awaken from this night of troubled dreams. But he did not need to pinch himself to know that it was Now, and Now was Real.

"Who is it that seeks to enter inside our gates?" another voice called out in the darkness.

"Arden Kendrick Hoffstetter, young and not so young. Child of misfortune," Belinda sang out.

The voice replied, "Let him pass."

Arden said then, "Go, and collect two hundred dollars," in a whisper which was ignored. He followed Belinda into another room.

He stood in a darkened basement, a damp chamber where bodiless half-faces emerged out of the blue shadows, featureless and remote. He had entered a tenement building with Belinda, had passed through a door, had been stopped by a voice from behind a screen and made to answer questions. He stood in a darkened basement room while he waited for the next display of multi-media dramatics. Belinda moved away from him and he stood alone, sweating uncomfortably, droplets of perspiration trickling down his chest and beneath his arms. The air was close and musty, unused and yet vaguely familiar, vaguely remembered.

"Do you know why you are here? Why you have been invited to join our brotherhood?" he was asked.

"I didn't know that I'd been invited. I thought I was ordered to attend," he replied, straining his eyes without success into the murk and gloom.

"The time-line approaches the point of maximum instability. From all points the shadows have amassed, congealing now before they are dispelled. It has been said by those who came before us that a free spirit emerges out of the darkness into the light as surely as the sun rises in the heavens. Hence the darkness which surrounds you now. Your trials have been many, but we have watched you along each step of the way. We see now, in the days ahead, in the light which is soon to follow, fame and success of great magnitude, fame and success which could very well have turned you against us.

"Therefore, we have invited you to join our brotherhood. You may never find love, but we will be here for you whenever you are in need. But remember, Arden Hoffstetter, the choice which you seem to feel has not been your own is, in fact, one that you yourself made many years ago, years before we had ever heard of your name. Think about this and be thankful."

Arden was pleased that someone had looked into his future, finding all those things toward which he had struggled. The room began to waver before him and he willingly acknowledged someone's hand on his shoulder. Comforting was the gesture, he thought. The shadows lifted, the air brightened and he saw a circle of somber but not unfriendly faces.

He was not surprised, for he had come to expect the presence of those he had seen and spoken to before. In gowns which assumed no earthly color, dark and indigo when the room had been shrouded in mystery, yellow and gold as the incandescent lights brightened overhead, he saw Belinda and Jeremy, Bernie Guysman and Mona Aikenclast, the redhaired subway murderer, Roosevelt Geldinger, the Ainu and others, faces he recalled from acid trips and office trips, summer excursions and winter diversions. They smiled now and he understood what was expected of him, all the reasons why he had been called.

"I cannot tell, can I?" he asked.

"No, never, never can you reveal what you have seen and heard. Others would come to try to work our magic upon themselves, others who care nothing for love, others who do not deserve. You know now, Arden, don't you?" Belinda replied for the group as every head nodded, all words agreed upon.

"Yet surely I would have stumbled upon you before too much longer," he went on. "When I reached my goals—isn't that so?"

"So and perhaps, maybe and maybe not. But do not trouble yourself too much about what the days ahead shall bring. We promise nothing. We only see what should be, what should become. We cannot guarantee life's uncertainties."

No longer couched in indifference, Arden's voice rang out. "And today, was today all planned? All of it? Even the business on the subway, even the interview and the cocktail party?" he asked them.

"Yes and no," said the man from the subway mayhem.

"Yes and no," said the head of Cerulean Studios.

"Yes and no," said Mona the Purple Prize.

"We cannot control your destiny. We cannot shape your moments of awareness. Either you are a creature of muscle and sinew, flesh and blood, or else you belong to the realm of ink and paper, promotionals and publicity announcements. We place ourselves, collectively, along the borders of your sight as you travel the currents of Time, and hope that you will do what is expected. You have not failed us, Arden Hoffstetter," said another voice, hidden and remote.

"You are Z, aren't you?" Hoffstetter asked, recognizing the voice from behind the screen and standing up on his toes but seeing nothing beyond the circle of unmoving heads and silent faces.

"I am that and all things. I was a friend of Fra Dolcino and Marguerite Porete, an admirer of naked Aegidius Cantor and the Homines Intelligentiae. But these things can all be found in books, and books hold life immobile, permanently trapped in time. I am the naked idleness of the spirit and I ask for nothing and no one.

"I am the fifth letter of our author's name. A riddle. A mystery. A striped creature hiding in a forest of religious fanatics, building towers which spiral with a poet's eye to meet the sun. A zany joke. A trauma and a bad dream from which there is no escape. Both the zenith and the bottomless pit of zero. A goof as you young people say. I can reveal no more."

"I don't understand."

Everyone laughed and Z told him, "There is no need for answers to questions which do not concern you, Arden K. Remember that and do not be troubled by ambiguity. It is all that we have left." The voice faded, hollow and growing ever more distant, like a record nearing its end, its last track or groove, until there was nothing, not even an echo.

"Have you found what you've been looking for?" Belinda asked him, moving from behind to lay over Arden's shoulders a robe which caught all the hidden meanings of a heartbeat.

"Yes." His voice was suddenly dry, quiet, and subdued. Tension released itself, floated overhead as his muscles relaxed and he wiped a hand across his brow.

"Tell us then."

Everyone waited with gleaming eyes and impatient lips.

"I am here," he began to tell them. "I have found the beginning of the trail which leads within my soul. I have arrived. For awhile, back there, you had me fooled and I thought that this was all a game, an author's wild vision or a canticle of fiction. I thought that there was nothing left to write about. But now I know better." He dropped his hands to his sides, gathered up the pieces of his composure which lay strewn about his feet like so many shoulder chips and tumbled dominoes. "I know better and I am far wiser for I have found what I have been looking for these past five years. I have found the perfect ending to my novel and I thank you."

THE END

> "The most authentic inside story of the
> big-time cocaine traffic that has hit print."
> *Publishers Weekly*

SNOW BLIND

ROBERT SABBAG

A BRIEF CAREER
IN THE COCAINE TRADE

From Amagansett to Bogotá, from straight to
scam to snafu then the slam, SNOWBLIND is
an all-out, nonstop, mind-jolting journey through
the chic and violent world of Zachary Swan, the
real-life Madison Avenue executive who em-
barked on a fabulous, shortlived career in smug-
gling——bringing better living through chemistry
from South American soil to New York nose.

"A MARVELOUS, CHEERFUL ADVENTURE OF
MODERN TIMES . . . ONE PART RAYMOND
CHANDLER TO ONE PART HUNTER THOMP-
SON."   *Washington Star*

"A FLAT-OUT BALLBUSTER . . . SABBAG IS A
WHIP-SONG WRITER."   Hunter Thompson

AVON/36947/$1.95

THE BIG BESTSELLERS
ARE AVON BOOKS

☐ **Lancelot** Walker Percy	36582	$2.25
☐ **Oliver's Story** Erich Segal	36343	$1.95
☐ **Snowblind** Robert Sabbag	36947	$1.95
☐ **A Capitol Crime** Lawrence Meyer	37150	$1.95
☐ **Voyage** Sterling Hayden	37200	$2.50
☐ **Lady Oracle** Margaret Atwood	35444	$1.95
☐ **Humboldt's Gift** Saul Bellow	38810	$2.25
☐ **Mindbridge** Joe Haldeman	33605	$1.95
☐ **Polonaise** Piers Paul Read	33894	$1.95
☐ **A Fringe of Leaves** Patrick White	36160	$1.95
☐ **Founder's Praise** Joanne Greenberg	34702	$1.95
☐ **To Jerusalem and Back** Saul Bellow	33472	$1.95
☐ **A Sea-Change** Lois Gould	33704	$1.95
☐ **The Moon Lamp** Mark Smith	32698	$1.75
☐ **The Surface of Earth** Reynolds Price	29306	$1.95
☐ **The Monkey Wrench Gang** Edward Abbey	30114	$1.95
☐ **Beyond the Bedroom Wall** Larry Woiwode	29454	$1.95
☐ **Jonathan Livingston Seagull** Richard Bach	34777	$1.75
☐ **Working** Studs Terkel	34660	$2.50
☐ **Shardik** Richard Adams	27359	$1.95
☐ **Anya** Susan Fromberg Schaeffer	25262	$1.95
☐ **The Bermuda Triangle** Charles Berlitz	25254	$1.95
☐ **Watership Down** Richard Adams	19810	$2.25

Available at better bookstores everywhere, or order direct from the publisher.

AVON BOOKS, Mail Order Dept., 250 West 55th St., New York, N.Y. 10019

Please send me the books checked above. I enclose $_____(please include 25¢ per copy for postage and handling). Please use check or money order—sorry, no cash or COD's. Allow 4-6 weeks for delivery.

Mr/Mrs/Miss _____

Address _____

City _____ State/Zip _____

BB 5-78

THE MONKEY WRENCH GANG

A novel by EDWARD ABBEY

AVON ⬢ THE BEST IN
BESTSELLING ENTERTAINMENT

A novel of great passion and eloquent rage by
"ONE OF THE BEST LIVING WRITERS."
Playboy

LANCELOT

THE NEW NATIONAL BESTSELLER BY

WALKER PERCY

 AVON 36582 $2.25

LANCE 5-78